THE
HOUSE
HUSBAND

JAMES PATTERSON is one of the best-known and biggest-selling writers of all time. His books have sold in excess of 325 million copies worldwide and he has been the most borrowed author in UK libraries for the past nine years in a row. He is the author of some of the most popular series of the past two decades – the Alex Cross, Women's Murder Club, Detective Michael Bennett and Private novels – and he has written many other number one bestsellers including romance novels and stand-alone thrillers.

James is passionate about encouraging children to read. Inspired by his own son who was a reluctant reader, he also writes a range of books for young readers including the Middle School, I Funny, Treasure Hunters, House of Robots, Confessions and Maximum Ride series. James is the proud sponsor of the World Book Day Award and has donated millions in grants to independent bookshops. He lives in Florida with his wife and son.

BOOK**SHOTS**

STORIES AT THE SPEED OF LIFE

What you are holding in your hands right now is no ordinary book, it's a BookShot.

BookShots are page-turning stories by James Patterson and other writers that can be read in one sitting.

Each and every one is fast-paced, 100% story-driven; a shot of pure entertainment guaranteed to satisfy.

Available as new, compact paperbacks, ebooks and audio, everywhere books are sold.

BookShots – the ultimate form of storytelling. From the ultimate storyteller.

THE
HOUSE
HUSBAND

JAMES
PATTERSON

WITH DUANE SWIERCZYNSKI

BOOK**SHOTS**

13 5 7 9 10 8 6 4 2

BookShots
20 Vauxhall Bridge Road
London SW1V 2SA

BookShots is part of the Penguin Random House group of companies
whose addresses can be found at global.penguinrandomhouse.com.

First published by BookShots in 2017

www.penguin.co.uk

A CIP catalogue record for this book is available from the British Library.

ISBN 9781786530981

Printed and bound in Great Britain by Clays Ltd, St Ives Plc

Penguin Random House is committed to a
sustainable future for our business, our readers
and our planet. This book is made from Forest
Stewardship Council® certified paper.

THE
HOUSE
HUSBAND

CHAPTER 1

I LOVE MY family. Truly, madly, deeply. But some days I could just…

Hey, I don't want to complain. It just gets hectic sometimes. What am I saying? It's hectic *all of the time.* Like when you're wrangling dinner for three hungry children, none of whom like to eat the same thing.

For instance, last month our oldest, Jordan, decided he was a vegetarian. It was family movie night, and we'd put in *Bambi.* Safe choice, right? Hah. When Jordan asked why that mean hunter shot Bambi's mother, we told him the truth (we always tell our kids the truth): the hunter was gathering food for his family.

Well, poor Jordie looked at us, looked down at the cheeseburger on his tray, then looked up at us again and said, "They ate Bambi's mother?!" And that was the end of meat for our oldest boy.

Our middle child, Jonathan, will only eat protein in nugget form. He doesn't care if it's processed or organic or even made of Bambi's mother. If it's a breaded nugget, he'll eat it. And nothing else.

As for our sweet baby Jennifer…well, she insists on feeding herself and the food usually goes everywhere except in her mouth. Her high chair ends up looking like a crime scene. It would be easier to drape yellow tape across it than to wipe it all down.

Somehow I manage to get enough nutrients into their young bodies to sustain life another twelve hours (that is to say, until breakfast), help the two older boys with their baths, hose down our baby girl in the kitchen sink, squeeze them all into jammies, crack open the adventures of Babar, Lord of the Elephant Kingdom, for story time, and then finally, at long last…bedtime.

But my day's not over. You're forgetting about the crime scene in the kitchen.

After sorting the dishes and wiping down all surfaces and taking Jennifer's high chair to a toxic-waste dump (where it will be buried for at least fifty-eight years before becoming safe for human contact), I gather up the trash and recycling and walk them out to the plastic bins behind our town house.

We're lucky enough to live a stone's throw from beautiful Fairmount Park and the Schuylkill River. Sometimes I put the kids in their coats and take them down to the river to watch the regatta teams pull and push their way around.

But proximity to the park means you get all kinds of critters creeping out of the woods. Such as squirrels, which love to gnaw at our plastic garbage bins. Fun fact: squirrels were first introduced to American parks right here in Philadelphia back in 1847. Someone decided that visitors to Franklin Square would be amused by the little buggers, so they released three of them, along with some food and nesting boxes.

Well, I'm sure squirrels were jolly fun back then, but today their descendants are brazen little jerks that chew through industrial-grade plastic to get to our garbage.

Which reminds me. I should have one by now.

I walk downstairs to our finished basement, and sure enough, there's a nut-brown squirrel angrily shrieking and bouncing around the wire cage. Well, Mr. Bushy Tail, maybe you shouldn't be breaking into people's garbage bins? After pulling on the rubber gloves and slipping on the breathing mask, I carry the squirrel to the back room with the furnace and the hot-water heater.

Once I close the door, the room is perfectly sealed; there's no way anything can escape—not even air. Which is the idea.

I turn the nozzle and listen to the gentle hiss. It's incredibly soothing. Mr. Bushy Tail has no idea what's about to happen to him.

Which is also the idea.

CHAPTER 2

TEAGHAN BEAUMONT HOLDS her baby boy and runs through her options.

She's already changed his diaper—twice. Offered him the breast, but he twisted away, grumpy. Given him a few drops of simethicone, in case he was suffering from gas pains. Nope. Perhaps he's overtired? Yeah, well, so is Teaghan. *Join the club, kid.*

Baby Christopher wails on and on, despite her strolling the length of their apartment with him nestled on her shoulder, cooing to him, singing to him. Though maybe Teaghan should stop that; her husband always says she couldn't carry a tune in a bucket.

"It'll be *okay,* tough guy," Teaghan murmurs over the baby's pitiful screams. "It'll be *okay.*" She's not sure if she's reassuring her son or herself.

It's 3:00 a.m., and in five hours Teaghan will have to return to the Job after six long, wonderful, wearying weeks of maternity leave. Technically, she's allowed eight weeks, but their savings account doesn't care about technicalities. They need her paycheck *now.*

Her husband, Charlie, is a freelance writer, and his paychecks come sporadically at best. And during these past six weeks, Teaghan doesn't think he's opened his laptop once. Not that she blames him. How could he concentrate on work when he has a beautiful new son in their apartment?

Charlie has always wanted a family, having grown up in a house full of rambunctious kids raised by loving, supportive parents. Teaghan's experience was somewhat, um, *different,* to put it lightly. Sure, a big family sounded fine in the abstract. Something to look forward to someday. In the meantime, though, Teaghan's Job was everything. Hell, she had a hard enough time fitting her husband into her schedule.

But Charlie reminded her that time was running out, and Teaghan knew he was right. Talk about a biological raw deal. Men could technically father a child well into their nineties, but forty-year-old women attempting to carry a child are considered "high risk." The phrase always bugged Teaghan. *High risk?* As if the contents of her uterus might explode?

"It's okay, little one," she murmurs. "It's okay. Your mommy might be losing her mind, but I promise, you'll be fine."

His cries bounce off the upstairs walls of their duplex brownstone apartment. Her childless hipster neighbors upstairs must be loving this.

Despite her advanced age of thirty-six, Teaghan gave birth to a healthy baby boy with ten fingers and ten toes and an amazingly powerful set of lungs. (Boy, can he yell.) Teaghan, however, didn't fare as well. She was forced to have an emergency C-section, which made her feel like an invalid and look like Frankenstein's monster from the neck down. She can't move without a surprising new pain popping up to say hello. And aside from the C-section scar, nobody told her about the swollen-breasts thing. Whoa, Nellie. They hurt even if someone *glances* at them.

But worst of all—and this is the thing that Teaghan never expected—she doesn't know how she's going to be able to leave her baby boy for eight or ten hours.

Separation anxiety has never been a thing in her life. She's never felt homesick. Sure, she loves her goofy husband, but if their paths don't cross for a few days, that's perfectly fine.

But the idea of handing her baby over and saying, *See ya in time for dinner feeding, kid…* it just feels insanely wrong. Every cell in her body seems to be screaming *NO! STAY HOME WITH HIM!*

But her time is up.

She walks baby Chris downstairs to their bedroom—in their carved-out piece of an old brownstone mansion, the living room and kitchen are upstairs, and the two bedrooms are in the basement. She gently nudges her husband with her foot. He groans but doesn't move. She nudges him harder.

"Come on, Charlie," she says, loudly, over the baby's wails. Charlie has the gift of being able to sleep through them. (Apparently, this is another genetic advantage afforded to men.)

"Nuhghhh," her husband replies.

"CHARLIE."

"Uh-huh."

"I need you to take him," Teaghan says. "I've gotta pump my breasts and clean my gun."

CHAPTER 3

RUTH, MY WIFE, finally arrives home at 8:20, which is a bit later than promised. Thank God the boys are already asleep. Otherwise they'd go rushing into her arms, like *Dad? Dad who?* But that's fine. What matters now is that she's home safe, and I'm finally able to squeeze in a little "me time."

The minivan is down the street; I got lucky earlier today and found a spot after a quick run to the supermarket. Parking on this block can be like medieval combat, and I hate to surrender the space. But what am I supposed to do? Stay cooped up in the house all night like a prisoner? No way. Togetherness is important to a healthy family, but so is time apart.

I navigate the narrow streets of Fairmount all the way past Broad, then turn right onto 10th Street. I mapped out the route online for optimal travel time—I don't have all night, after all— and this seemed to be quickest.

Still, I'm a dad in a minivan, so other drivers see me as an obstacle to speed around, not a fellow commuter. It's like *Mad Max* out here, with me fighting them block to block. Things are a bit easier once I cross South Street and I'm out of Center City altogether.

That said, parking in South Philly is even more of a nightmare than it is where I live. I circle a few times, straining my eyes as I hunt for a space big enough to park this child-friendly behemoth. What makes it difficult is that I'm near the narrow and clogged streets of the famous Italian Market, where Rocky Balboa once ran. After spending twenty minutes winding through the neighborhood, it becomes very clear why Rocky didn't bother to drive.

Finally, I catch a glimpse of a battered Jeep pulling out onto the street. I hammer the accelerator and make it there before anyone else. However, this is not exactly a space meant for a minivan. I'm not even sure how the heck the Jeep fit here. Somehow I defy time and space and squeeze myself in. I look at the street signs and realize I'm four blocks away from where I'm headed. Which is not necessarily a bad thing, but again, I don't have all night.

So I hurry a bit as I peel off my mock turtleneck and khakis and pull the uniform over my body. My belly's a little bigger than I'd like. Sure, I have a six-pack, but it's sort of buried under another six-pack, or maybe even a half case. But if you eat enough meals standing up over a sink—usually whatever the kids didn't finish— you're going to grow a gut. Maybe tomorrow I'll take the kids to the park and run around with them. Let Jonny sit on my shoes as I crank out a few sit-ups. It'll probably make him giggle to see Daddy huffing and puffing.

Uniform finally on, I take my clipboard and tool bag and walk down Christian Street. While the Italian Market is only a few blocks away, this part of South Philly is relatively quiet, especially on a late fall night like this. I double-check the address on the clipboard, then knock on the insulated front door.

"Yes?"

The woman who answers is Donna Pancoast, thirty-five, and the first thing I notice is that her eyes are a little puffy. Maybe from crying. Maybe from drinking. I'll know soon enough, I guess.

"PGW, ma'am," I say, trying to suppress the urge to giggle. "Your radon detector isn't working, I understand?"

PGW is short for the Philadelphia Gas Works. Everybody knows that gas is silent and potentially deadly. Nobody wants to take any chances when it comes to a leak or a faulty detector.

But Ms. Pancoast here has no idea what I'm talking about.

"I didn't call the gas company."

"Is your husband home?"

The look in her eyes confirms everything. The mere mention of the word *husband* causes her eyes to dim a little bit. She's been crying. And drinking, too. I can see the almost empty carafe of red wine on the dining-room table.

"Ray!" she calls back into the house. But she also steps aside to allow me to enter.

I'm telling you, it's the uniform. Give yourself a slight air of authority, and people will pretty much let you do anything.

CHAPTER 4

THE HOUSE IS one in a row, one of the older types. Native Philadelphians call them row homes, though technically they should be called row houses. A house is a building; a home is a house with a family inside it. The distinction is important. Nobody says, "There's no place like *house*."

And indeed, this home contains a family. They're all in separate rooms, of course, lost in their individual pursuits. Dinner was most likely consumed separately, too, which is a shame. You don't know how much it kills me that my whole family is only able to dine together on weekends, but that's out of work necessity. With the Pancoasts, it's a matter of choice.

Donna calls up to her husband again with more irritation creeping into her voice.

"Ray, would you please come down here now!"

"All right, all right, what's the matter with you?"

When Ray comes down the stairs, I can understand why his wife resorts to excessive drinking. He's a squat, hulking boar of a man and even uglier in person than he is in the newspapers.

"Mr. Pancoast, your radon detector is malfunctioning. Could you show me downstairs so that I can give you a replacement?"

"I didn't call about a faulty radon detector. Think you got the wrong house, buddy."

"We check them wirelessly now," I lie. "One of our trucks drove by earlier today and picked up the alert."

Note: I am completely making this up. Gas companies don't do drive-bys checking for faulty equipment. Then again, I'm not dealing with a brain surgeon here, either.

Pancoast eyes me up and down for a minute, then decides I'm no kind of threat.

"Yeah, come on, I'll show ya."

I follow him down into the cramped basement, which is a mess. As he walks toward the gas meter, I pull a pipe wrench out of my tool bag, making sure there's just the right amount of space between us. Too far, I'll miss. Too close, I won't be able to swing properly.

"Right over here."

"Where?" I ask, pretending I don't see.

I squeeze tight on the pipe wrench and prepare myself. He's just a big squirrel. A 240-pound, hairy squirrel with a beer belly and halitosis.

"Right there, what are you, bl—"

Metal connects with skull, and it's good night, Mr. Pancoast. He collapses to the ground with all the grace of a sack of potatoes being heaved onto a locking dock.

"I'm not blind, Ray," I whisper, even though he can't possibly hear me. "I see everything, as a matter of fact."

It's not hard to find the correct pipe. One thing about Philadelphia row houses: they're reliably predictable.

I slip on my breathing mask and prepare to do my thing.

CHAPTER 5

THE WHOLE THING takes less than an hour and a half, start to finish. How that's for efficiency?

When I pull up to my block, my original spot is gone, of course. But look! There's an even better spot open, closer to our house. The parking gods are smiling upon me. Sure, this is a good omen.

It's after 10:00 p.m., and Ruth's already in bed, with Jennifer curled up close to her. I almost hate to disturb them. As quietly as I can, I strip out of my clothes (don't worry; the PGW uniform is hidden away where no one can find it) and slip under the warm covers. I feel Ruth stir a little. Sweet little Jennifer, meanwhile, is dead to the world, God bless her.

"Sorry to wake you," I whisper to my wife.

Ruth murmurs something that sounds vaguely like English but on further analysis may actually be 100 percent gibberish.

"You can sleep in a little later tomorrow," I tell Ruth. "I know you had a hard day at work."

Another murmur. Perhaps she's saying *Okay?* Or *Amen?* It's hard to tell.

"I'll get the boys to school and bring this little animal here along for the ride, okay?"

Even though she doesn't reply, Ruth tucks her body closer to mine.

I put my hand on her hip and give it a gentle squeeze. "Sweet dreams, honey," I whisper. I kiss her head, taking in the scent of her shampoo. Somehow, even after a day in the city, her hair is always intoxicating to me.

We fall asleep together, and I revel in the peace and comfort of it all. I hope the Pancoast family is enjoying a similar kind of peace.

CHAPTER 6

FOR TEAGHAN, SIX weeks away from the Job feels like six years. Even the most ordinary routines (the morning briefs over pitifully bitter coffee, checking their vehicle out of the motor pool) all feel like things she did in another life. Is she really a homicide detective? Or is this a dream she's having after being up way too late with the baby, watching bad cable TV?

No, Teaghan knows it's all real. She's been a homicide detective for three years, all of them partnered with Martin Diaz, who's always been a laid-back, supportive partner. Until this morning.

"Hey, T," he says. "How's the little one?"

"Adorable, but he kind of screams all the time."

"Yeah, that sounds about right. You getting much sleep?"

"You're a dad. What do you think?"

"I think this is going to be a very long day for you."

Teaghan invited Diaz and his wife over to meet the baby, but Diaz begged off, saying he didn't want to bring germs into their apartment and get the little one sick. Teaghan had to admit she was a little hurt. The Diazes were like family. But she didn't push it—maybe the germ thing was a real concern.

But now Diaz didn't seem exactly thrilled to have his old partner back. Teaghan was gone for six weeks. She had her belly cut open and a new life form airlifted out. And all she gets is a *Hey?*

Whatever. Maybe she is reading too much into things. Maybe Diaz has always been a bit distant and Teaghan just doesn't remember.

The first case they catch: a multiple homicide in South Philly.

Diaz looks at Teaghan with concern and asks, "You sure you're up for this?" It's something he never would have asked before.

"Yeah, Diaz," she says. "I had a baby. I'm not going through chemo."

"No, yeah, I mean…" He trails off, fumbling for the words. "It's a whole *family* we're talking about here."

"I've seen dead kids," Teaghan says, which is sadly true.

Diaz is in the driver's seat for a change, even though he's a lousy driver. The doc told Teaghan she should wait at least six weeks before getting behind the wheel, so why push it? She grudgingly agreed. Besides, she was so sleep-deprived she felt like a zombie shambling around in the haze of the newly resurrected. Diaz might treat stop signs like mere suggestions, but at least he's had his solid eight hours of pillow time.

The weird thing is, their drive over to Christian Street is deathly quiet, as if they're sitting in a church pew waiting for services to begin. Is Diaz seriously pissed at her or something?

In her absence, Diaz was shackled with another detective, a burnout named McCafferty, which couldn't have been fun. (McCafferty's idea of proper homicide investigation is to glance at the scene of the crime on her way to the nearest bar.) Teaghan is sure the past six weeks were a huge frustration for Diaz. But does Teaghan deserve the silent treatment for that?

Maybe it's something else. Diaz wasn't shy about his opinion when Teaghan told him the supposedly joyous news. "Popping out a kid is gonna hurt you," he said, and he didn't mean it in the literal sense. Diaz meant that it would hurt her career.

Which made Teaghan angry, because plenty of homicide guys had kids, and no one ever gave them grief about it. She supposes it's okay for a cop dad to be gone all the time, working murders nonstop. But if a cop mom does the same, then whoa, there's something seriously wrong here. Where are her priorities?

"Something wrong, D?" Teaghan asks.

It's *D* when she's talking to him human-to-human and *Diaz* when it's cop-to-cop.

"You mean aside from the fact that we're about to walk into a house full of dead people?"

"Come on, you know what I mean."

"I'm fine," he says, making it sound like a sigh. "Why?"

"You seem unusually quiet."

"Been a tough couple of weeks, that's all."

"Yeah, and I missed you, too."

Diaz grunts as they pull up to the death house on Christian Street. "I'm sorry, T. I guess I'm just not looking forward to what we're about to see."

Truth is, neither is Teaghan.

CHAPTER 7

THE PANCOAST FAMILY died together yet all alone.

A classmate of the oldest Pancoast child called it in; she thought it was weird that nobody responded to the front door at 7:30 a.m., when the house was usually at its busiest. And their car was still parked in their painted-off disabled spot—a perk someone on City Council threw Mr. Pancoast years ago (even though he was far from disabled).

The first responders knocked aggressively, kicked in the door, and made the awful discovery. Word travels at lightning speed in tight-knit South Philly neighborhoods like this. Everyone within a four-block radius knew what had happened to the Pancoasts by the time the Homicide Bureau did.

But that is what puzzles Teaghan and her partner. This sounds like a horrible accident. Why are they tagging it a homicide?

Teaghan pulls herself out of the passenger seat, trying not to let on how much it hurts. Her stomach muscles seem to be screaming at her, *We can't move this way anymore!* Ugh, it feels like she is being torn in half.

"Ready, Diaz?" she asks, trying to deflect attention away from her own miseries.

But even a distracted Diaz can't help but notice that his partner's in pain. "You're not going to get morning sickness on me, now, are you, T?"

She would have ordinarily replied with a creative expletive, but there are lookyloos and TV reporters all over the place.

The Pancoast residence is a narrow, deep row home, just like the others on this block. Teaghan doesn't know how people can stand living on top of each other like this—hell, even her apartment feels bigger—but she guesses it saves on the heating bills in the cold, bitter Philadelphia winter.

The mother is in the living room, her body twisted up over the shattered remains of a wineglass. The CSI tech on duty tells them she died of asphyxia, but that is pretty obvious to both of them. Both Teaghan and Diaz have seen it plenty of times before.

Teaghan wants to crouch down to take a better look at the mom's face, but that would most likely end in agony or embarrassment. So she tries to get what impressions she can from a standing position.

It's clear that Donna Pancoast was pretty once. Take away the bluish tint of her skin and the extra pounds from drinking too much, and it's not hard to see the beautiful young bride beneath.

Don't judge, T. You used to be young and pretty once, before the Job and the baby and the Frankenstein scar took all of that away.

So what went wrong? Why all of these worry lines on the

woman's face? Why the dark circles under her eyes, like she'd been drinking her days away?

"There are three kids?" Diaz asks.

"Upstairs," says the CSI tech. "Each in their own room. Two of them were on their cell phones; the other was doing homework. It looks like they just went to sleep."

"What about the dad?" Teaghan asks.

"Well, that's why we called you guys," the CSI tech says.

CHAPTER 8

DAD IS DOWN in the basement.

Head hanging low, sitting next to the furnace, as if he fell asleep trying to keep warm on a wintry night.

His skin has the same awful blue tint as the rest of his family. But unlike the rest of his family, his body language suggests he wasn't caught unaware with a sudden flood of natural gas throughout the home. He wasn't having a drink or checking a social-media site or doing homework. Ray Pancoast was just sitting here, waiting for the dark veil to fall over his eyes a final time.

"Man," Diaz says, then catches himself.

"You think he did this?" Teaghan asks.

The CSI tech uses a badly gnawed pencil to point to a small square resting next to the body. It's a piece of notepaper torn off a pad from the Hyatt at the Bellevue Hotel on South Broad Street, a venerable Philly institution—but also infamous for the outbreak of so-called Legionnaires' disease back in 1976. Thirty-four people died thanks to bacteria in the hotel's air-conditioning system.

Now, there's a bad omen, Teaghan thinks.

Diaz crouches down to read the note. "'I'm sorry,'" he reads aloud. "'I should have been a better father.'"

So this isn't an accidental death. This is a suicide-quadruple homicide.

But something about the whole thing doesn't sit right with Teaghan. She may not be the world's quickest detective, but she is one of the more methodical ones. She thinks it through, step by step, and realizes there's a big hole in this theory.

"You're saying the husband opened up a pipe, flooded the whole house with gas."

"That's what it seems like," the CSI tech replies.

"So why couldn't the family smell the leak?" Teaghan asks. "I thought the gas company puts in a rotten-egg odor so you can tell when there's a leak. Didn't any of them realize something was wrong?"

"Ah, see, that's the clever part," the CSI tech says. "The husband not only opened up the pipe, but he had some kind of filter device on there to take away the mercaptans—that organosulfur compound you're talking about. My guess is the family had no idea."

"No signs of trauma?" Teaghan asks. "Maybe somebody forced him to do this."

The CSI tech points to the back of Pancoast's head. "Well, there's a nasty contusion on the back of his skull. But that could be because he was writhing around a little toward the end and banged his head on the wall."

"You find traces of his blood anywhere else? Or on any tools?"

"Nothing yet. Just the wall. But don't worry, I'll luminol the heck out of the area and let you know if anything turns up."

"Yo, lemme talk to you for a minute," Diaz says, tugging on Teaghan's arm.

"What is it?"

"C'mon."

Up in the kitchen, away from everybody else, Diaz tells her he recognizes the dad, Ray Pancoast.

"Which means?"

"He's the boss of the steamfitters local."

"And?"

"Come on, T, these are the Philly unions we're talking about. You've been in the city long enough to know what that means. Dad was probably up to some dirty business and found himself tap-dancing on the edge of an indictment. Instead of facing the music, he decided to take the coward's way out and took his family along with him."

"Amazing," Teaghan says. "You just tried and convicted a man based on his street rep and a single sheet of paper."

"Naw, we'll do our thing. I'm just giving you a sneak preview."

Teaghan knows Diaz is probably right. Yeah, she has been in this city long enough to know better. But pushing aside the cop inside her, the human part of her can't wrap her mind around it. What could possibly compel a man to snuff out his entire family? You spend years raising, clothing, feeding, protecting, and loving these little people, and one day you just decide to hit the reset button and wipe them all out? None of it makes sense.

"I don't know, D," she says. "Seems a little extreme to me. I mean, his wife and kids…"

"You're new to the joys of being a parent," Diaz says. "Call me in a few years when you're pulling your hair out and putting yourself to bed with Jack Daniel's. You'll get it."

Diaz is married with kids and often seems to regret both parts of that description. Not that he complains overtly. It's the little things he says, especially when there's a family gathering on the horizon. There's also his reluctance to report right home after a shift. More often than not, he's stopping off at McNally's in Fox Chase, not too far from home. As if he needs some kind of boozy buffer before walking in his own front door.

Teaghan doesn't understand it. Then again, she's been a parent for all of, what, six weeks now? Maybe that's what happens.

"Come on, Diaz. Let's step outside for some fresh air."

CHAPTER 9

YOU WOULD THINK watching a crime scene would be exciting—at least, that's what all of those psycho-killer-of-the-week shows on TV lead you to believe. But in real life, they're seriously kind of boring. Lots of people standing around, wondering if they're going to see a real dead body. TV news reporters and cameramen, wondering if there's a place nearby with a decent hot pork sandwich.

My Jenny doesn't mind, though. She's strapped to my chest in one of those kangaroo-pouch things and giggling in all the chilly air and sunshine.

"What the heck happened over there?" some old guy asks me. He has enough hair growing out of his ears to blend in with his sideburns.

I cover little Jenny's ears with the palms of my hands. She thinks I'm playing a silly game and giggles even more.

"They found a dead family in there," I whisper.

The old man is more curious than horrified. "Dead? Dead from what?"

"This isn't official," I say, "but they think the father gassed his family to death."

At this point, Jenny starts to fuss. Can she hear my words through my hands? Does she know enough words to understand what I'm saying?

God love him, the old man takes this news in stride.

"Ah, this crazy town." As if such a thing is a normal occurrence here in the birthplace of our nation. He swats at an invisible fly, then continues down the block.

I coo at Jenny, rocking her gently. "You're okay, baby doll. Daddy's here. Don't listen to that old man. You're growing up in a safe place."

We watch the scene for a while longer. I wonder if we should head home. Jenny's going to need to be changed and have her lunch soon. But some hunch tells me to stick for a while longer. And ten minutes later, my intuition is rewarded.

Two people step out of the Christian Street house. There's a squat Latino guy in a sports coat and a tall red-haired woman in a button-down shirt and loose-fitting slacks. He looks bored. She looks like it hurts to walk.

They're homicide cops. I'll bet anything on it.

My homicide cops.

You can tell they're homicide cops because they look like they tour war zones on a daily basis and are in charge of racking up the body count. I'd never want a job like theirs. Too depressing, too pointless.

The way they talk to each other indicates they're deep into something. But what? You'd think the case would be open and shut. A father decides to spare his family a lot of grief and ends their time on earth.

But the pretty red-haired one…yeah, there's clearly something bothering her.

"Isn't there, Jenny? Look at the lady policewoman. She looks awfully worried about something. Wonder what's on her mind."

Her Latino partner looks like he's carrying a heavy burden, too.

"And poor Mr. Policeman doesn't look like he's having much fun, either. I wonder why. Do you know, Jenny?"

If she does, Jenny's not letting on. She squirms impatiently and fusses some more.

I'm too far away to hear exactly what they're talking about, but I catch enough words to get the gist. *Pancoast, unions, you know this city.*

What kind of detectives are you guys? Are you the never-stop-until-we-get-our-man type? Or are you a bit more laid-back, ready to believe anything the CSI techs tell you?

Speak of the devil, after a while the CSI guy sticks his head out the front door and summons his colleagues.

"Detectives Diaz and Beaumont? You got a sec?"

"Diaz," I tell Jenny. "Do you know how to spell Diaz? Daddy does. It's D-I-A-Z…"

CHAPTER 10

THE DAY TEAGHAN thought would never end finally does. She even splits a little early, which earns a raised eyebrow from Diaz. Whatever. Like he's never bounced ahead of schedule, leaving Teaghan to finish some last bits of paperwork?

Whatever.

Back at their West Philly apartment, Charlie hands off the sleeping baby as if Christopher is a bomb he just painstakingly defused.

"The only way I could get him to stop crying," Charlie whispers, "was to keep walking with him. Back and forth, up and down, all over the place. My legs are killing me."

"Did you try the bouncy seat?"

"Yeah, and that didn't do a thing to help. I just think he missed you."

And I missed him, too—like you couldn't believe.

Charlie seems eager to get back to his laptop; he hasn't written two coherent words all day. (Nor has he showered, apparently. Her husband looks like an unmade bed.) But Teaghan also needs a moment. She can't exactly breastfeed with a gun strapped to her torso.

Of course, the moment the baby realizes that he's in his mother's arms, he starts to fuss and pout, which only intensifies as he wakes up. Teaghan is exhausted and sore; she thought she'd have a few minutes to relax before becoming a walking food source.

"You got him?" Charlie asks. "I'm sorry, but I really have to get back to this article."

"Go," Teaghan says. "I'll be fine."

She's lying, but that's what keeps couples together sometimes. The well-placed lie.

It's hours before little Christopher calms down again. Ordinarily, after a tough day, she and Charlie would knock back some craft beers while waiting for the delivery guy to show up with their dinner. Now dinner is a lukewarm vegetarian stew, eaten over the sink while gently rocking the baby. No beer for the homicide cop now. Whatever Teaghan eats, the baby eats, and the last thing she needs is a cranky drunk on her hands. She dealt with enough of those early in her career.

But Teaghan doesn't fully ease back into full-time mom mode. Part of her brain is still in detective mode, too, and can't help thinking about the Pancoast murders. She's been on the Job for ten years, on homicide for the past three, and can't remember a case quite like this.

"Hey, sweetie," she coos. "How about we do a little googling?"

An hour later, Teaghan is still holding the baby while she reads up on *familicide,* the word for the type of murder or murder-suicide that results in the death of at least one spouse and one or more children. Yeah, she didn't know the word, either. But now that she does, she can't seem to shake it loose from her mind.

Familicide. Sounds like a poison you use when a family is infesting your home.

Cases of familicide are rare. But surprisingly, they're also the most common form of mass murder—even in this age of psychotic people carrying assault rifles into churches, clinics, schools, and movie theaters.

Baby Christopher stirs a little. But it's not Mommy who replies; instead, it's Detective Beaumont, who really doesn't want to be interrupted right now.

"Shhh. Not now, kid."

With one hand, Teaghan does a news search for Philadelphia and familicide cases over the past five years. No hits—which is good news. But then she thinks about it. How many reporters would use the word *familicide* in a tabloid newspaper? A lot of reporters she knows don't even get name spellings right. So she tries a search with *Philadelphia, mass murder,* and *family.*

Tenths of a second later, Teaghan is shocked to see there were not just one but *two other* cases of familicide in Philadelphia. And both happened in the past six weeks, when she was out on maternity leave.

"No way," Teaghan says.

The hard edge in her voice startles the baby, who erupts into a full, panicked wail.

CHAPTER 11

WHEN YOU'RE COOPED up in the house all day with three life-forms under the age of ten, the internet can be a godsend.

Yeah, I'm a stay-at-home dad whose wife works in a big, important office downtown, but it wasn't always this way. I used to be a normal guy who liked to socialize with humans over the age of ten. I liked to gossip about work, and I enjoyed discussing how badly the Eagles were doing. I still crave shallow and mindless human interaction.

Which is why the gods gave us social media.

I don't have many actual, true-blue, known-'em-since-kindergarten friends on Facebook. But the weird thing about Facebook is that you can pretty much be the Unabomber and end up with hundreds of "friends." People see you comment on a buddy's site, decide you don't look and talk like a troglodyte, so they'll toss you a friend request. I almost always accept, unless the "friend" looks suspiciously like a single lady from overseas searching for a husband. Job filled and then some, thank you very much.

No, what I crave are details about other people's families. They can make you feel better about what you're doing—or infinitely worse.

You know what I'm talking about, don't you? C'mon, who hasn't felt that burning envy when you see a "friend" and his family enjoying some lavish all-inclusive vacation on a Caribbean island? Or sitting down to a mouthwatering meal at an exclusive, pop-up, one-time-only restaurant run by a celebrity chef? Or engaging in some wild family sport like extreme caber tossing? (Hey, say what you want about the Scots, but any sport where you have to wear a skirt strikes me as extreme.)

Then there are the other posts. The ones that make you feel sad, because some families…well, they're stumbling.

Or downright failing.

It's amazing what some people will share online.

Like the stay-at-home mom who complains about having no sex life and jokes with her friends about having an affair with one of the young trainers at the ten-dollar-a-month gym she visits every morning after dropping the kids off at school.

Or the married father of four who posts crude pornographic and racially insensitive jokes for his buddies. What happens when his daughter (Hannah, fourteen and cute, even in braces!) goes online and sees them?

Or the workaholic, depressive mother of two who goes on and on about how she has no time for anything anymore. Hey, Mom, here's a tip: stay offline and maybe enjoy your kids a bit more!

People are crazy, I'm telling you.

Sure, we all make mistakes. But what really bothers me is when innocent children get caught up in those mistakes. When I hold my baby girl, it hits me how defenseless she is. How she looks to us for everything, including her basic survival. What happens to babies who have royal jerks for parents? Or worse, older kids with awful parents who will someday grow up to be awful parents themselves, perpetuating this endless cycle of…

Ah, listen to me. I don't mean to get on the soapbox. I'm just trying to make the point that I don't go on social media merely for the vicarious thrill. I'm worried about the families out there. So I scroll through post after post, looking for a family who might need my help.

And thanks to my trip to the crime scene this morning, I might have lucked into one.

The best part about social media is that it's not like you're watching a movie or a ball game. I can dive in for six minutes—or sixty, depending on how my day is going. Because one moment you're wrapped up in someone else's life, and the next you've got a child tugging on your sleeve, begging (whining a little) for you to head outside and roll a soccer ball at him a million times.

Like right now.

Yes, Jordan, Daddy will be more than happy to help you with your kicks. This old man still has a few tricks up his sleeve.

CHAPTER 12

SECOND DAY BACK on the Job, and it's no easier for Teaghan to leave her baby boy at home with her husband.

"Daddy will take good care of you, sweetheart," she says softly. "You guys are going to have a good time."

Baby Christopher, however, doesn't buy it. He responds with a new, pitiful round of shrill cries.

"I know, baby. Your mommy's sad, too."

The ache is not just emotional. It's physical, too. Her swollen breasts seem to want to feed her kid all the time. (At least today she remembers to pack her breast pump. And she doesn't care if Diaz gives her grief about it, either.) Her arms want to hold Christopher close, even though they're still sore from holding him in the middle of the night, and the weight on her body inflames her C-section scar, too. Motherhood—whatever doesn't kill you makes you tired.

But at least this morning she's leaving their brownstone apartment with two addresses and a purpose.

Namely, to figure out why there's been a weird uptick in familicides here in the City of Brotherly Love. Did someone dump something in the water supply while she was on leave that made everyone go insane?

The first address takes Teaghan to the Brewerytown neighborhood, a rapidly gentrifying area on the fringes of a not-so-great one. She squeezes into a parking spot on Girard Avenue, then walks up to the town house.

The area is probably no more dangerous than her own in West Philly on the outskirts of Penn's campus. But Teaghan's out here without her partner, and the last thing she needs is to get blindsided. Once a city girl, always a city girl. You never, ever let your guard down.

The neighborhood borders Fairmount Park, which is a bonus, and a lot of the row homes are big, with sturdy bones. Some urban professionals have been taking a chance on these kinds of places for years. You buy it cheap, fix it up, and hope the next hot new neighborhood springs to life around you.

That was probably the strategy of successful Center City defense attorney W. Harold Posehn. He could have afforded any place in the city, probably even swank Rittenhouse Square. But he and his wife, with their three kids, opted for this big town house on a quiet street just off Girard. And they probably enjoyed it. For a while.

Six weeks ago, however, Posehn's wife drowned all three of their children in their claw-foot tub—including an infant—before stabbing her lawyer husband with a butcher knife. Then she slashed her own wrists, lay down next to the bodies of her dead children, and waited for life to fade away.

Teaghan shudders just thinking about it. And she's not the kind of cop to shudder over a multiple homicide.

And now here she is, visiting the scene of the crime just a month and a half later.

The town house is still vacant, of course. Tough enough to sell a place this deep into Brewerytown on a good day, let alone one that was the site of a horribly violent crime. Earlier this morning, Teaghan called the Realtor, who grudgingly gave her the punch-in code for the front door. "Aren't you people done with this place yet?" he complained. "I swear, it's nonstop with you guys." Teaghan bit her tongue and thanked him for his patience.

Now that she's on the front stoop, however, she finds herself wishing she'd never called in the first place. What does she hope to gain by seeing the murder scene?

She punches in the code. The lock beeps twice. She turns the knob and opens the thick, heavily insulated door into a shockingly large living room. Though the interior has been stripped bare, it's clear the Posehns put a lot of work into the place. This is exactly the kind of place she'd love for her, Charlie, and the baby someday.

There's a tool bag and a small wastebasket with junk-food wrappers and soda cans inside. The Realtor must have hired somebody to make the place immaculate again. Which only makes Teaghan realize she's procrastinating. What she came to see is up a flight of stairs.

The master bathroom, where it all happened.

Ordinarily, it would be the kind of space any homeowner would dream of—pristine tiles, a huge double sink with a wide mirror and state-of-the-art fixtures. But the centerpiece is the claw-foot tub, big enough (Teaghan swears) to fit a small vehicle.

But this is no dream room anymore. This is the scene of a nightmare.

Teaghan can't help herself. She kneels down on the hard tile (which is remarkably clean) and reaches out to touch the tub. They truly don't make them like this anymore. The porcelain enamel is chilly under her fingertips. She can feel the unforgiving strength of the cast iron beneath.

When they thrashed, did they feel the horrible, unyielding weight all around them? There was nowhere to go. Not down, not to the side. And up above was the person who was supposed to love them and protect them, but she was holding them down, her arms like iron, too…

No.

Teaghan can't do this.

She stands up and sprints back down the hall. She half stumbles down the flight of stairs and makes it out the front door just in time to vomit on the sidewalk.

A second wave of nausea overwhelms her, which doesn't make sense, until a moment later, when it's followed by sharp, stabbing pains throughout her torso. For a few minutes, she's not sure she's going to be able to stay conscious. The world swims around her.

Don't push it, the doc said. And here she is, doing the exact opposite.

CHAPTER 13

TEAGHAN IS FEELING better by the time she makes it over to the scene of the second familicide.

By "better" she means it doesn't hurt quite as much to breathe. But she's afraid to look at her belly scar for fear of what she'll see down there.

This neighborhood, Chestnut Hill, is a far cry from Brewery-town. This is the place to live when you can afford Rittenhouse Square but prefer a more suburban feel within the city limits. Politicians, professors, doctors, and lawyers have called this neighborhood home for generations. Even James Bond lived here. (Well, the ornithologist, after whom Ian Fleming named his famous spy.)

But all of that class doesn't mean Chestnut Hill residents always behave.

Three weeks ago, a sixty-year-old society matron named Eleanor Cooke decided to spike some soup with arsenic and serve it to her husband and four children—two of them grown adults—at their weekly family dinner. After Eleanor watched her family struggle, writhe on the floor, and finally die, she apparently took an overdose of painkillers to end her own life, while an LP of classical music played in the background. The fourth movement of Tchaikovsky's Symphony no. 6, to be precise. It was allegedly still playing when responding officers kicked down the front door hours later.

The tabloid report didn't mention what kind of soup she served.

But the reporter did detail the Cooke family's squabbles over inheritance money, which was the source of much local gossip over the years.

That is probably why the Realtor hung up on Teaghan when she called earlier this morning to ask about gaining access to the home.

But Teaghan doesn't need to see the kitchen or the dining room to know that something's *off* here. As she stands in front of the $3.3 million Bells Mill Road spread (seven bedrooms, eight bathrooms), she finds herself wondering why Mrs. Cooke would decide to end the family line right here on a chilly Sunday evening.

It doesn't make sense. You spend your life building up all of this—the family, the estate, the cars, the possessions—only to wake up one morning and decide to blow everything out of existence with a pot of soup?

What *mother* could ever do that to her babies, even if they were grown-ups and behaving like brats?

Teaghan looks up at the house, struggling to wrap her mind around it.

What if it wasn't Mrs. Cooke? What if someone read the same tabloid report Teaghan did and was inspired by the Brewerytown killings to settle an old grudge?

CHAPTER 14

I'M NOT TOO proud to admit it.

Sometimes you just have to bribe them.

When I pick Jordan and Jonathan up from school (a private Quaker institution, just as our Founding Fathers intended), I promise to take them for frozen yogurt *if*—and *only if*—they'll stay quiet while Daddy takes them for a short drive.

They happily agree. Even baby Jennifer—clearly following the lead of her older brothers—seems to add her consent. Adults may be addicted to things like alcohol and nicotine, but nothing gets kids jonesing like the promise of a little fro-yo with as many toppings as they want. (Well, within reason.)

In truth, the drive is pretty far from home, all the way up in a corner of the city that I don't know too well. The phone's GPS tells me it can take up to forty-five minutes, depending on traffic. And the best route is along the infamous Roosevelt Boulevard, which is a twelve-lane highway of sheer mayhem. It makes me nervous to be driving on it with the kids. But any other way will take forever, and my bribe—no matter how sweet—has its natural limits.

Fox Chase is in Northeast Philadelphia, home to a lot of cops, firefighters, and blue-collar workers. I never thought my adventures would lead me up here, but hey, sometimes you can't predict how life will go, you know?

Fox Chase is surprisingly nice and clean, with a few single homes scattered among the twins. The family I'm curious about lives in one of the singles, a three-bedroom rancher, definitely within the range of the husband's salary. They look like they live comfortably. There are toy trucks and little action figures scattered on the front lawn and a swing set out back. I drive around the block a few times, and I admit, I'm pretty jealous of the yard.

But like any parent knows, appearances can be very deceiving.

Because if my internet research is right, then the husband has been messing around with a coworker. The wife knows, sadly, but she bottles it up and takes her frustration out on her kids. Which is not cool. At all.

I think I'm going to have to pay them a visit tonight, after my own wife gets home. The drive up Roosevelt Boulevard shouldn't be too bad after 9:00 p.m. And if I tuck my revolver away in the back of the car ahead of time, that should save me a few minutes.

But first, as promised…

It's time for some fro-yo, kids!

CHAPTER 15

AT LONG LAST, baby Christopher goes down for the count. Maybe even for longer than thirty minutes this time. (Who knows? Miracles do happen.) And Charlie's downstairs pounding away on his laptop, so he won't be up to bother Teaghan, either.

She takes advantage of the silence (however brief it may be) and pumps some breast milk. She's almost used to the whirring and sucking and wheezing of the machine, so much so that if she's not paying enough attention, her milk will overflow. Which is a huge pain, not to mention sort of embarrassing.

But Teaghan's got enough of a handle on it that she can focus on some work while she supplies tomorrow's baby buffet. She places her laptop on the kitchen table right next to the breast pump and wonders what her grandmother (God rest her soul) would think of this setup. *You need two machines to feed your baby? What madness is this?*

Yeah, it all seems crazy to me, too, Nana.

Teaghan scrolls through online articles about the Fairmount and Chestnut Hill murder-suicides, hoping to stumble across a detail or two she missed on her first read. She doesn't want to go requesting the case files unless she has something solid. Otherwise, she's just sticking her nose into somebody else's case, and no detective likes that.

Logically, Teaghan knows that the cases are very different. There are no obvious social or business connections between the Cookes and the Posehns, the methods vary, and the motives appear solid—horrible as they might be. Still, Posehn was a Center City lawyer and most likely traveled in well-heeled circles. It's not inconceivable that someone in the Cooke family orbit would have known him personally. Did Posehn's death somehow expose a deep, dark Cooke family secret? And someone decided the whole tribe had to go?

Or is Teaghan trying to force a connection where there is none?

She glances down at the pump. *Whir, suck, wheeze.* Her milk drips into the collection bottle. Doctors say it's the sweetest, most nutritious liquid in the world.

Mother's milk.

Did Eleanor Cooke think about mother's milk as she served her four children that awful Sunday evening? She was a mother, after all, who fed her babies and watched them sleep and get sick and recover and eat and grow. How could she bring herself to place a bowl full of poison in front of them and watch them lap it up?

Stop it, Teaghan tells herself. *Stick to what you know.*

And statistically speaking, what Eleanor Cooke did made sense.

If you are murdered, there's a 50 percent chance your killer will be somebody you know. Sometimes it's a member of your own family. During her years on the Job, Teaghan's seen enough domestic-violence cases that went right up to the edge and, if not for cooler heads prevailing or a knock on the door, could have gone real ugly.

Maybe Eleanor Cooke was pushed to the edge. Posehn's wife, too. You never know what secret wars people are fighting.

But still…something feels *off* to Teaghan. Especially when she adds the Pancoast family to the mix.

What are the chances of three familicides within a two-month time span?

As she ponders, Teaghan gradually becomes aware of a sound, possibly in another apartment. Someone crying. A baby. Wailing. Geez, it's almost 9:00 p.m. Won't somebody pick the kid up and make it stop crying?

It's only when Charlie emerges from the basement with a still-sobbing Christopher in his arms that Teaghan realizes…

Oh, hell, that was my *baby.*

CHAPTER 16

"HEY," CHARLIE SAYS. "Didn't you hear him?"

"I was catching up on some work, and I still have more to do. You got him for the time being?"

A slightly pained look washes over Charlie's face. "I've been with him all day. I was trying to catch a few hours of sleep so I could get my brain working again. I've only got a few days to finish that Manayunk piece, and they're going to look at me like I'm crazy if I ask for another extension."

"Yeah, well, I have work tomorrow morning, too. And I can't just blow it off when I feel like it."

Charlie recoils as if he's been slapped by an invisible hand. "What the hell is that supposed to mean?"

Teaghan realizes that her words were a bit harsher than intended. "Nothing. Never mind. I'll take him."

Christopher's sobs increase in volume and intensity, as if he can understand exactly what his parents are saying.

And with his cries Teaghan feels the tug on her body. Her breasts suddenly feel like they're about to burst. It's really strange.

The homicide cop in her wants to keep poking and prodding to find the secret connection between these three cases, but the mom in her wants—no, *needs*—to feed her baby *right now*.

"Give him to me," she says, struggling to detach the pump without spilling milk all over herself.

"No," Charlie says, "I've got him. You finish up. After all, you're the one with the real job."

"I never said that. Damn it, Charlie…"

But her husband takes her baby back downstairs to their bedroom to try to get him back to sleep.

Way to go, Teaghan. You won the battle, but your breasts feel like they've lost the war.

Maybe that's it—maybe her hormones are so far out of whack that she's seeing connections that aren't really there. She can't remember feeling this way about any other case. Teaghan operates on facts, not hunches. Hunches are for TV cops.

She thinks about going downstairs, taking the baby, and just giving him the breast already—and giving Charlie the break he clearly needs. Putting the cases on ice until tomorrow morning. It's only her second day back on the Job. What, did she expect to crack this one sitting at her kitchen table?

Except…

Except that whenever a detective is in doubt, you talk to your partner. That's why God (or at least the police commissioner, which may be the same thing) sends you out into the world in pairs.

Teaghan listens until she's sure that Charlie and the baby are out of earshot. Then she plucks her cell phone from the kitchen table and enters Diaz's number. It's still early, especially for Diaz. How many times has he talked about staying up past midnight because that's the only time he gets to enjoy a quiet house?

But after a few rings, Diaz doesn't answer. Great.

Is her partner still angry because she took maternity leave? If so, well, *way to be passive-aggressive, buddy.*

CHAPTER 17

WIFE HOME.

Boys and baby tucked in.

Time for a little "me time."

When Ruth asks where I'm headed, I tell her.

Well, I don't tell her *exactly* where. That would violate the idea of "me time," right? The little mysteries are what keep a marriage alive.

So I tell her I'm headed to Lucky Strike to bowl for a while, which gives me an excuse to go to the closet for my bowling bag. I don't have to search too hard, because I pulled the bag out earlier this afternoon while Ruth was still at work and got everything ready.

I'm a man with a plan. Always have been.

There is one sticky detail about tonight's work, however: the odometer on the minivan.

A drive down to Lucky Strike in Center City is barely a mile; my actual destination is about thirteen miles away. Which means I'll be adding at least twenty-six miles to the number, not just two.

Now, my darling Ruth is hardly ever in the minivan. Even when she is, I doubt she bothers to eyeball the digital odometer. Sure, it's a small detail, but I really hate loose ends. Because what if one day she *does* happen to notice? And she thinks I'm having an affair or something? (When I could possibly have time for an affair is a question for a physicist, because it would require violating the space-time continuum.)

As I'm fretting over this and pretending to search the closet for my bowling bag, Ruth asks if I wouldn't mind picking up a few things from the Wawa on the way home. Fresh milk for the kids, maybe some oranges and bananas? I smile, stand up, tell her no problem, then kiss her on the forehead. I tell her she can have anything she wants. Which is the truth.

She smiles at me sweetly, then goes off to take her nightly bath.

I put the bowling bag on our bed and unzip it. My actual bowling ball—a Christmas gift from three years ago—is hidden behind some shoeboxes in the back of my closet. Instead, the bag contains a revolver, which I purchased this morning from a dealer on Spring Garden Street—the same place where a lot of Philly cops shop, as a matter of fact.

Which is kind of funny, considering.

CHAPTER 18

EVERY FAMILY IS unique and demands its own personalized instrument of doom. When the kids are older, we'll play *Clue,* and I'll teach them this important lesson.

Take Colonel Mustard, for example. He's modeled after the classic British imperialist, a bushy-bearded military man of means. So a candlestick or a lead pipe just won't do. No, this Great White Hunter deserves death by something more fitting, like a revolver. Or, even better, strangulation by rope. Fun fact: his name is a reference to the horrible choking gas used to kill hundreds of doughboys in World War I.

Not that I'll necessarily tell my children this.

Anyway, when I selected my current target, I knew I had to up my game.

For a lying, corrupt union man like Pancoast, carbon monoxide was the clear choice. Let him choke on the toxic fumes that run throughout the pipes of the city he fleeced. For a rich bitch like Eleanor Cooke in Chestnut Hill, I needed poison to fill all of their bellies, just like they poisoned each other with incessant greed over the years.

But tonight a gun seems to make the most sense.

Because my target is a police officer.

D-I-A-Z.

CHAPTER 19

DETECTIVE MARTIN DIAZ comes home late so often he genuinely can't remember the last time he came home on time. Or what that even felt like and what he used to do when he got there.

Family moments seem to happen by accident, in passing. It's what his wife has come to expect, and so have his kids. They understand Daddy's a homicide cop, which means strange hours and long nights. And usually a moody dad the next day, especially if the case was particularly gruesome.

But over the past two months, the nights have gotten even later. And every time he sets foot in his own house, it looks more and more foreign to him, like he's accidentally let himself into his neighbor's place. Is this really his sofa? All of the food in the fridge—is that his, too? Who eats all this stuff?

Diaz pushes his key into the front door and flips the dead bolt, then steps inside, trying to make as little noise as possible. He doesn't want to wake anyone up, because this is his transition time. A little quiet as he goes from being a murder cop to being a husband and father who's very skilled at avoiding his family.

In fact, Diaz is so used to opening the door into an empty living room that it genuinely takes him by surprise when he sees his whole family—Franny and the three kids—sitting there around the dining-room table in the dark.

"Close the door," a voice says.

Who the hell is that?

Diaz squints until he sees the silhouette of a stranger now visible. And he's holding something to his wife's head. The blood in Diaz's veins runs ice-cold. This can't be happening. Not to him, not in his own home. This is the dark, awful stuff of nightmares. It's not supposed to happen in real life.

Then Diaz reminds himself: *I'm a police officer. I'm the guy you call when faced with situations exactly like this one.*

"We don't have much," he says, "but you're welcome to whatever you like. I'm not going to stop you."

"Shut up," the voice says, "and close the door."

Diaz complies, pushing the door shut with a calm, fluid motion to let the stranger know that he's not going to try any funny business. This is most likely a home invasion, takeover-style. Not unheard of but unusual up here in the near-suburbs of Fox Chase. Most times, you have idiots knocking over the row homes of drug dealers, expecting to walk out the front door with either product or cash (or both).

"It's gonna be all right, Franny," Diaz says, reassuring his wife that he's in charge.

Franny says nothing. She just stares at him, frozen in shock.

"You're out quite late, Detective," the voice says. "Didn't your shift end hours ago?"

"So you know I'm a police officer."

"Of course I do."

"Then you probably realize how foolish this is."

"I've had a gun on your family for the past hour. Who's the foolish one in this situation? Mmm?"

Diaz struggles to see exactly who he's dealing with. Is it just this punk, or does he have accomplices elsewhere in the house?

The closer Diaz looks, however, the more he's confused by the situation. This guy doesn't look like your usual street tough in a hoodie or a junkie aiming to snatch your silverware so he can buy a baggie of heroin. Maybe his eyes are playing tricks on him, but to Diaz, this guy looks like Mr. Joe Average White Dude.

"Tell me what you want," Diaz says calmly.

"I want you to tell us where you've been since the end of your shift."

"You don't know anything about me or my job."

"Your partner, Detective Beaumont, that's B-E-A-U-M-O-N-T, reported home on time. But then again, she's a new mother. I suppose she hasn't had time to grow bored with her spouse."

CHAPTER 20

THE REALIZATION IS like a slap in the face. This is no punk, Diaz thinks. This guy has been stalking him. *Both* him and T. But how? And more important, *why?* Even worse, the guy seems to know one of Diaz's guiltiest secrets. That crack about the spouse can't be random.

So there's no choice, Diaz decides. There will be no talking this guy down from the ledge. He's come here for something, and it's not the silverware.

Diaz reaches for his gun, but Joe Average presses his weapon to the side of Franny's head.

"Don't," he says, almost like a bark.

His whole family jumps. His baby daughter starts crying. Oh, hell, the children. Not that Diaz has forgotten about them. He's just been praying like crazy that they could be magically whisked away from the scene, safe and unharmed. His twin boys and his baby girl.

Diaz immediately shows the stranger his palms. "Look! I'm un-armed. Don't hurt them, please."

"You're the one who hurt them, Detective."

"I don't know what you want."

"To make things right."

The more Diaz looks at the guy, the more he thinks he knows him. Okay, maybe *know* is too strong a word. But there's something familiar about him.

Meanwhile, Joe Average pulls the gun away from Franny—but then points it at the back of his daughter's head.

"Please!" Franny cries out. "Don't! You said you wouldn't hurt them!"

"And I won't," the stranger says, "if you do exactly what I say."

Franny nods.

Diaz can't stand this. He so very, very badly wants to run toward them and leap over the dining-room table, tackle this monster, and pummel him to death with his fists. But Diaz knows he can't possibly move fast enough to stop a bullet. And no matter what stupid things he's done over these past two months, his family's safety will always—always—come first.

Part of his brain—that very small part that's still in active cop mode—picks away at the stranger's face. Diaz knows he's seen him before. But where? Was this some guy who caught a glimpse of him (and his badge) at a bar one night during the past few weeks? Put it all together?

"Mrs. Diaz," the stranger says.

Franny does not respond. It's as if she's retreated to some other mental space. Maybe she thinks she's dreaming, too.

"Franny."

It makes Diaz furious to hear him use her first name. But this seems to snap her out of her shocked state.

She gasps. "What?"

"I want you to walk over to your husband and take his service weapon out of its holster."

Franny slowly stands up, her joints clearly stiff from sitting and panicking for who knows how long.

"Now, Franny. I haven't got all night."

"Okay, okay."

The blood in Diaz's veins is running red-hot now. This guy, telling his wife what to do. It's killing Diaz, because the guy's face is familiar from somewhere. If he could just figure out *where,* maybe he'd have a shot at disarming him somehow. Turning the tables.

Franny clears the distance between the table and her husband. Diaz keeps his hands away from his body to allow her easy access to the gun. It's a strangely intimate moment. His eyes search for hers, but Franny refuses to look at him. Either she can't, or she won't.

Diaz feels his chest tighten. This can't be happening. Why is this man doing these horrible things to his family?

"That's it," the stranger says. "Unbutton the safety strap, and take it out."

She does.

"Now, take a few steps back."

She does.

Wait.

Family. The very word jogs a memory in Diaz's brain. He remembers the last time he saw a family in this kind of situation. And they were all dead from carbon-monoxide poisoning in separate rooms in a house on Christian Street in South Philly. Teaghan knew something was funny about that crime scene. If only he had listened to her instead of trying to lecture her.

"Now, I want you to point it at your lying, cheating husband."

"What?"

At that moment, Diaz remembers. He knows where he saw the stranger's face.

"And shoot him in the heart."

CHAPTER 21

BOY, THIS HAS been an uncomfortable couple of hours.

I really thought Detective Diaz would have been home a lot sooner. I mean, how long can an extramarital dalliance take? What, did they stop for pizza and milkshakes afterward?

I swear, I didn't mean to snoop into his personal life. I was simply curious about the two homicide detectives tasked with the Pancoast case. Were they smart cops? Lazy cops just showing up for the paycheck? Not that I was all that worried. I had thought everything through to the smallest detail. I'm a full-time stay-at-home dad; I have to be a detail man.

And part of that attention to detail is knowing who it is you're up against.

Detective Teaghan Beaumont is apparently just back from maternity leave, which explains the way she moved at the Pancoast crime scene. And the beautiful glow in her cheeks—only new moms have that kind of radiance. I remember how sore Ruth was after each of our children was born; it's a heck of an ordeal, natural childbirth.

But I also remember how beautiful she was.

With his partner off to become a mom, Detective Diaz was temporarily partnered with one Theresa McCafferty, who was three years older and a shameless boozehound. Also a shameless flirt.

Most cops knew to steer clear of this particular train wreck. But Detective Diaz, well, I suppose he felt he was owed some attention. Anyone else might find Detective McCafferty a bitter pill to swallow. But to Detective Diaz, she was just what the doctor ordered.

How did I learn all of this, you ask?

Fair question.

Sure, I'm a stay-at-home dad. But I used to have a job outside the home, and I still have contacts in that world. Which come in handy from time to time. (Plus, Facebook is great at filling in the gaps.) And let's just say that Detective Diaz wasn't doing much to cover his own tracks.

The thing is, Detective Diaz soon began an ill-advised and very public affair with Detective McCafferty. Perhaps they thought they were safe, carrying on in cop bars and at McCafferty's Northern Liberties apartment. But the thing about cop bars is, they're full of cops.

And cops really like to talk.

I'll admit it—I immediately felt horrible for the Diaz family, even though I hadn't met them until the moment I knocked on their door, presenting myself as a police department counselor with a very urgent matter to discuss. Mrs. Diaz was all too eager to grant me access to her home, offering me a seat and a cup of unsweetened iced tea.

You see, I had to intervene, because I knew exactly how this would all play out. At some point, Mrs. Diaz—Franny—would learn about the affair, and she would either (a) soldier through the faithless marriage for the kids' sake or (b) divorce her cheating husband for the kids' sake.

But what she wouldn't realize is that the kids would be the ones to suffer no matter what option she chose. Detective Martin Diaz would already have damned them. They would grow up to repeat the same mistakes as their parents, and the cycle would continue forever.

Unless someone could do something about it.

A man with a plan.

Now Franny Diaz has a gun on her husband, and she's most likely thinking about what I've told her during the past hour, because she asks him, "Is it all true, Martin?"

The twin boys are old enough to know what's going on. They stare at their father with a delicious kind of hate even more intense than their mother's. The little girl, mercifully, doesn't seem to know too much about what's going on. Her only response is to sob gently.

Don't worry, angel. It'll all be over soon.

"Franny, please…"

"Is it?" she demands.

But the answer's already in her husband's eyes.

And now Francine Diaz is pointing the gun at her husband like she really means it.

CHAPTER 22

TEAGHAN IS COMPLETELY lost in her case notes when her cell phone finally rings. What is it, close to midnight now? She snatches the cell off her kitchen table, already annoyed.

"Took you long enough, Diaz."

The voice on the other end, however, is not Diaz. It's someone female, her voice slurring a little as she speaks.

"Detective Beaumont?"

"Yeah, who is this?"

There is an audible sob, then the sound of a deep breath. "It's Theresa. From Homicide. We met a bunch of times…"

Teaghan puts it together quickly: Theresa McCafferty, Diaz's temporary partner. If they were back in high school, McCafferty would be the kind of insufferable bully who would go out of her way to snub and embarrass Teaghan. Only this isn't high school, and both of them carry badges and guns. Those "bunch of times" they met weren't pleasant; Teaghan tries to steer clear of cops like McCafferty.

"Yeah, I remember. What's up?"

It's strange to hear McCafferty sound so sad, so…vulnerable. Cops like McCafferty don't do vulnerable.

There's a long pause before she finally asks, "Did you hear about Martin?"

"No, what happened?"

And then everything seems to rush at Teaghan all at once. First, it's Charlie, carrying their sleeping baby in his arms, a stricken look on his face, coming up from their basement bedroom.

"T, I'm so sorry. I just heard about it on WHYY…"

But Teaghan is confused. Sorry about what? Has the entire world lost their minds at the same time?

"What are you talking about?" she asks.

And then her cell phone buzzes—another call coming in. McCafferty, meanwhile, is still on the line saying something about Diaz and his family, all of them, even the kids, and God, she's so sorry.

"McCafferty, tell me what's going on!"

"They were shot, Teaghan. In their own home. Just a short while ago. Oh, God, I can't believe it…"

None of this makes any damn sense to Teaghan…

Charlie, looking at her like she's just received a diagnosis of terminal cancer…

McCafferty, going on and on about the whole family being butchered…

The other call, buzzing again, insisting on breaking through…

And then she gets it.

The realization hits her like a sledgehammer to the chest, and Teaghan starts sobbing, right there at her kitchen table. Her fingers scratch at the case notes on the tabletop.

My God.

Diaz.

The baby, following his mother's cue, wakes up and does the same.

CHAPTER 23

CONFLICT OF INTEREST can take a flying leap; Teaghan demands access to the Diaz house *now*.

The uniforms guarding the perimeter take one look at her face and realize they'd be fighting a losing battle. One of them lifts the yellow tape and allows her through.

It's 3:00 a.m., and the streets of Fox Chase are still pitch-dark. But neighbors up and down the street have emerged from their warm homes to take a look for themselves. Clearly, they've all heard the horrible news. Their shocked faces are illuminated by the red and blue lights from the squad cars as they look around and huddle for warmth and safety.

They all must know the Diaz family—know the father was a homicide detective. Usually, with a cop living on your block, you feel a little bit safer. But when the same cop is killed along with his family, what does that mean for your own family?

Teaghan walks up the front pathway, steeling herself for what she's about to see inside. Didn't she and Diaz just do this a few days ago?

You sure you're up for this?

Yeah, Diaz. I had a baby. I'm not going through chemo.

No, yeah, I mean…It's a whole family *we're talking about here.*

I've seen dead kids.

But Teaghan has never seen dead kids she knew.

Teaghan and Charlie have visited the Diaz house at least a half dozen times over the past couple of years. (Their family get-togethers had to be at the Diaz place; the Beaumonts' cramped apartment wouldn't work.) Charlie loved playing out back with the Diaz boys, kicking a soccer ball around and roughhousing, while Teaghan and Martin would knock back a few beers and talk a little shop. Or at least as much shop as Franny could tolerate.

Come to think of it, those visits to the Diaz home were probably what gave Charlie the baby itch. They'd spend their drive back to West Philly debating the pros and cons of starting a family. Charlie, naturally, had plenty of items in the pros column (*we're not getting any younger, I've always wanted a big family, look how much fun we had today*), leaving Teaghan to fire back all of the cons (*we both have demanding jobs, their place is too small, life is crazy enough without the burden of raising a kid*).

But in her mind, they all boiled down to one big con: being a parent means you're responsible for another life. And that can be a terrifying thing. Charlie still doesn't get that. He hasn't been to the dark places that Teaghan has been to in her life.

Like this one.

Teaghan takes a deep breath and steps through the front door.

Come on, T, she tells herself, *you've been to dozens of crime scenes. You know what to do.*

But another voice shoots back: *Yeah, but it's never someone you know.*

CHAPTER 24

INSIDE, THE FORENSIC team is still at work, but everybody sounds pretty confident about what happened. Teaghan heard it on the drive up to Fox Chase, straight from the chief of the Homicide Bureau.

In short, Detectives McCafferty and Diaz were having an affair. She couldn't believe it. *Her* Diaz—her partner, her rock—and that hot mess, carrying on like a couple of teenagers? "McCafferty pretty much admitted the whole thing," the chief said. "Now she's afraid someone's gonna come after her." Apparently, it's been an open secret in the Homicide Bureau. Teaghan hadn't heard because she'd been busy having a kid.

Somehow poor Franny Diaz found out about it. Probably not from another homicide cop; the blue wall of silence was formidable. (Even if Teaghan had known, she's pretty sure she'd never tell.) Most likely, Diaz himself slipped. Left behind the wrong bar receipt or forgot to delete a text.

No matter how it happened, Franny reached her breaking point. And tonight, after Diaz returned home, Franny took her husband's service revolver and shot him with it, twice in the chest.

Then she turned the gun on her children, swiftly, before taking her own life.

Which…*no.*

Teaghan refused to believe it, even if the physical evidence was right there before her very eyes.

Her partner, dead on his own living-room floor, two shots delivered right to his chest, both in the kill zone. Cops are trained on silhouettes to shoot with maximum stopping power. So are many cops' wives, Franny Diaz included.

The Diaz kids—all three of them—were sitting at the kitchen table when they were executed.

And then Franny apparently went into the kitchen to take her own life, as if she couldn't stand the sight of her husband any longer.

Except…

Except this makes no sense *whatsoever.*

Teaghan spent many hours with Franny. Ending her children's lives was absolutely the last thing she would ever do. She was the kind of mom who would single-handedly lift a tractor-trailer off the family car if it meant she could protect her babies. Teaghan considered her a role model, in fact, for how to be loving yet tough as steel. She wanted to be Franny when she grew up.

And Franny wasn't some fragile flower who would become unhinged at the news of Diaz's infidelity. Hell, on the force, that is practically an epidemic. Quickest way to ruin your marriage? Put on a badge.

No, Franny Diaz would have given her husband holy hell, then taken off with the kids and immediately hired the toughest divorce attorney she could afford. She wouldn't end Diaz with two taps to the rib cage; she'd make him suffer for the rest of his days. That's the kind of woman she was. Not a killer. Not a suicidal head case.

A flash snaps Teaghan out of her thoughts. One of the CSI guys is taking a photo of something near Diaz's body. A shell casing, maybe?

"What's that?" she asks. "By the hand?"

Calling it *the hand;* distance is the only way to get through something like this.

The CSI guy looks up at her, recognizes her, then mumbles his apologies as he moves out of the way.

Teaghan can't crouch down, but it's plain as day from her standing position. A word, scrawled in blood, right near Diaz's hand. Written in his own blood on the living-room carpet:

DADDI

With the last letter only partially formed, because Diaz most likely died while writing it. Her partner's final will and testament: *Daddy.*

CHAPTER 25

WELL, TONIGHT HASN'T gone as planned.

At all.

I drive home feeling pretty low, to be honest. The problems were twofold: my target and my choice of weapon. In other words, maybe I made a mistake messing around with Colonel Mustard and the rope.

That is to say, Detective Martin Diaz and a gun.

Cops are always problematic because they keep such weird hours. When I discovered that Detective Diaz was having an affair, I thought it might be an occasional fling, not an every-night-I-can-get-away bender. So there I was, sitting in his house, holding his wife and kids at gunpoint, for, like, well over an hour. Talk about awkward! The poor kids, up way past their bedtime, watching their mother with increasingly panicked looks in their eyes. I'm telling you, if Detective Diaz hadn't finally arrived home when he did, I think the situation may have spun out of control on its own.

(Say what you will about the Cookes, but at least they had their Sunday dinner at the same time, without fail.)

And then there was the math of the situation. If one—or all of them!—decided to rush me, I'm not sure I could have pulled the trigger. Because I'm not a wanton killer. If the deaths can't be arranged just right, I won't go through with it. I deliver peaceful mercy, not terrifying death. They might not all have appreciated the nuances in the moment, but I'm sure they'll all understand in the afterlife.

Where everything will make sense to all of us.

Forever and ever, amen.

So anyway, I've got all of this nonsense swirling around in my head as I make the long drive back to my neighborhood. I'm so preoccupied I realize I've forgotten to pick up the milk, oranges, and bananas Ruth wanted from the Wawa. Wonderful. Not that she'll complain. Ruth's not the type. But the slightly disappointed look in her eyes will be punishment enough. She will have to make an extra run to the store, which will make her workday all that much longer. And the last thing I want to do is make her life more difficult.

As I pull up to our block, I think about heading out to a twenty-four-hour market anyway, but then I see there's a parking spot open not too far from our front door. I can't leave it to chance. If I don't take the spot now, someone else will. I'll just have to deal with my wife's disappointment tomorrow.

I'll also have to come up with an explanation for why I was out so late tonight. A man can only bowl for so long, and again, I don't want her to start to worry. Or to think I was being a dirty dog like Detective Diaz.

I guide our minivan into the space, cleanly, expertly. You live in Philadelphia long enough, you can almost parallel park on autopilot. But this time—whoa—my back right tire bumps into the curb, jolting me in my seat. What the heck? I must be losing my touch.

I change gears, pull the minivan forward a few inches, cut the wheel a little sharper, and try again.

And this time, BUMP, again.

This is insane. I reach for the gearshift, slide it from R to D, checking the display to make sure I'm not in the wrong gear or something. That's when I notice the odometer.

Now, when I left earlier this evening, I was careful to note the number of miles on there. (Always do.) It was 56,702.

I calculated the drive to Fox Chase and back in advance. The journey should have only added 26.5 miles to the count. Roughly a marathon. If I were in much better shape, I could have theoretically run up there and back.

So why does my odometer read 68,791?

CHAPTER 26

THE DEPARTMENT GIVES her a few days off, which are both welcome and awful.

Because Teaghan's only been back on the Job, what, a couple of days? And now she's back in her apartment in mom mode again. The cop part of her brain is pissed off. *What the hell is this nonsense? I want to work.*

Need to work.

Charlie is no doubt secretly thrilled. Teaghan can mind the baby while he really drills down into his Manayunk piece. "You should enjoy the extra time with the little guy," he says. "He's what's important now."

And she knows her husband didn't quite mean it this way, but what about Diaz and his family? Are they no longer important?

So she says nothing.

But the cop part of her brain is screaming. The cop part of her brain wants justice for her fallen partner. For Franny. For the boys. And his little girl.

Teaghan holds her baby boy, rocking him gently, trying to get him to stop crying and go to sleep for just a little while so she can think.

"Shhh, now, sweet thing."

The whole thing is so coincidental as to be absurd. A homicide cop is involved in a murder-suicide at the same time as he's investigating another murder-suicide? Even before she heard the news, Teaghan thought the first three cases of familicide were about two too many. Now there's a fourth, just days after the Pancoast murders?

But what is she really thinking? That somebody is going around murdering innocent families and trying to make it look like they did themselves in? That is equally crazy.

"You're okay, little guy. Shhhh, now. Mommy's here, Daddy's here, everything will be all right."

Except...

Except that one word hangs her up: *innocent.*

Were these four families actually innocent? As much as it pained her to admit it, Martin Diaz certainly wasn't. Playing around on Franny behind her back, and with that drunk McCafferty, no less. The chief almost didn't have to confirm it; the shock in McCafferty's voice said it all. And it explains why Diaz was so weird and chilly with her on her first day back. You can't fool a fellow detective for long. Sooner or later, Teaghan would have found out, and he'd have had to deal with her wrath. She might not have ratted him out to Franny, but her partner had to know Teaghan wouldn't put up with his duplicity for very long.

The chief said it was an open secret in the Homicide Bureau.

But if there *is* some killer out there, targeting whole families, does that mean the killer is a cop? A horrifying thought, but who else could have known about Diaz and McCafferty?

And what's the connection to the Pancoast murders, for that matter? Or the others?

Maybe Pancoast was guilty of something, too. That's what Diaz himself alleged back at the crime scene.

Come on, T, these are the Philly unions we're talking about. You've been in the city long enough to know what that means.

So the killer knows about Diaz's dirty business and Pancoast's…What about Cooke and Posehn? What was weighing on their guilty consciences?

Baby Christopher refuses to go down without a fight—he's just as stubborn as his mother. As he continues to cry with increasing intensity and her breasts ache, Teaghan considers tearing Charlie away from his computer, just for a few minutes, so she can think.

But no. That would be admitting a kind of defeat. She can be a homicide detective and a mother at the same time, can't she?

So she'll just suck it up and ignore the wailing.

Teaghan's mind goes back to the Pancoast crime scene. Are there any physical similarities between that and the Diaz scene? Killers typically follow a pattern, even when they're trying hard not to follow a pattern. She needs something tangible to connect the two. She can't walk into her chief's office with a well-intentioned *hunch*.

Teaghan mentally runs through both crime scenes, as if flipping the pages of two different photo albums, looking for a detail to repeat itself.

"Shhh, honey, everything will be okay. Mommy's on the case."

And then it suddenly hits her, the connection between the Pancoast and Diaz murders. *Duh!* It's so obvious she chides herself for not hitting on it hours ago.

The link between the two cases is Martin Diaz.

CHAPTER 27

THIS MORNING, I feel like the last man on earth.

I'm sitting alone in my quiet, empty house. Not completely alone, of course; Jennifer's tucked away in her crib taking a nap. But the boys are at school, and Ruth isn't returning my texts—or my calls, for that matter. Is it about the forgotten bananas and milk or something more? She was arctic-cold to me this morning. I tried to apologize, explaining that I didn't realize how late it had gotten, but she didn't even want to have the conversation. Wonderful.

Nothing makes a husband feel quite as miserable as the silent treatment.

So now I'm sitting here, writhing in my own self-loathing, thinking about how I can make it up to Ruth. Maybe if I run to the grocery store and gather up the ingredients to prepare her favorite dinner (shrimp and basil linguine)? Yeah, that's definitely the way to go.

This will also give me an excuse to double-check the odometer on the minivan. Maybe I was seeing things last night. That, or baby Jennifer is sneaking out at night to go joyriding.

But when I reach the minivan, I realize two things. I've forgotten my keys. And more important, I've forgotten baby Jennifer, who is still sleeping upstairs in her crib.

Crapsticks!

I pound the fat of my fist against the passenger-side window. How could I be so stupid? I pound again and again, grunting with every blow. Sometimes I could just…

Passersby give me hard looks, like, *Who is this lunatic?* Sorry, folks, just a harried house husband, losing his mind a little. Go back to your own perfect lives, and let me have a meltdown in privacy.

Well, standing out here beating my car up isn't going to help anything. So I trot back up the stairs to my front door and punch in the access code, and…

BEEP BEEP.

Nothing. Red light blinking.

Huh. Must have punched it in wrong. I try again.

BEEP BEEP.

Red light blinking.

What the…?

The access code is our anniversary, month and year. Not something I'd ever forget. But this stupid security door seems to have forgotten. What, does everybody have it in for me today?

BEEP BEEP.

Red light blinking.

If I try the code again, the security company will be alerted, which means the alarms throughout the house will freak out, and the police will be summoned. And maybe I'm just being silly and superstitious, but it seems like a supremely bad idea to call the cops the day after you've killed one of them.

But I can't stay out here on my stoop. Not with Jennifer inside alone. What if she wakes up and starts to panic because her daddy's not there (because he's a bonehead)?

Think, *think*...

Now, I *could* walk down to Ruth's office in Center City and grab her physical house keys. But that would take at least thirty minutes round-trip—and that's if my slightly out-of-shape (to be honest, gone-to-seed) self ran most of the way. Yeah, that would be real charming, showing up at Ruth's workplace, saying *Sorry*-huff-*dear*-huff-*I*-huff-*seem-to*-huff-*have-for*-huff-*gotten*-huff-*my*-huff-*keys*...

No way.

Besides, Ruth would be furious with me if I left our baby girl alone in our house for a half hour, all because I left in a hurry. (Never mind that I was in a rush because I wanted to extend an olive branch in the form of her favorite dish ever.)

Standing out there, on my stoop, I realize I'm going to have to do something absurd.

Break into my own home.

CHAPTER 28

AN ADULT HOMEOWNER spends a lot of time thinking about how to make the ol' homestead burglarproof. Ruth and I were very good at this. We sat down and made a list of everything we wanted: motion detectors, frame and floor bolts for the front and back doors, and bars on all of the basement-level windows.

Which, of course, makes the task at hand fairly difficult.

How the heck am I going to break into the domestic equivalent of Fort Knox? I stare up at my own house, completely flummoxed.

Then I turn to look down my block and see it, a furry little rodent with a bushy tail darting up the trunk of a hardwood tree. My old nemesis, the common gray squirrel.

That little creature gives me the answer I need. Because when I engineered my little squirrel trap in the back of the house, I removed the bars from the window. So all I have to do is go back there, push the trap into the house, then shimmy my way in. Which I do, feeling like a complete outlaw (and moron).

The trap falls to the linoleum basement floor with a terrific clatter. If the neighbors don't hear it, poor baby Jennifer certainly will.

I rip the hell out of my shirt and pants as I climb through the basement window. And let me tell you, there is no graceful way to make it to the floor. I drop and stumble and fall on my butt. The Olympic judges don't even bother to raise their score cards.

I climb up the stairs, listening for Jennifer's cries. But I don't hear her at all. How could she have slept through the sound of the cage banging off the floor? But I do hear a noise upstairs. Something like…running water. Did I leave a faucet running, in addition to forgetting my keys?

I pick up my pace and run through my living room. Strangely, there's a tool bag on the living-room rug, next to a small mesh wastebasket overflowing with junk-food wrappers and soda cans. Where did that stuff come from? Did Ruth and the boys have a party last night?

Never mind that now. I need to check on that running water sound, which seems to be coming from the upstairs bath. Horror and panic grip my heart. There's no way Jennifer could crawl out of her crib, make her way to the bathroom, and turn on the faucets…is there?

I run up those stairs faster than I've ever run before and practically hurl myself down the hallway and into the master bath. The door is partially open. I kick it so hard it bangs against the wall.

Inside our bathroom is an image I can't quite comprehend at first.

We have a massive claw-foot tub, which practically persuaded us to buy this home right on the spot. And now the faucet is running full tilt, and the tub is filled to the brim and overflowing, the fluid slapping onto the tile floor in gushing waves.

But that's not water in the tub.

My God, is that…

Blood?

CHAPTER 29

"LET ME SEE the crowd footage from the Pancoast case," Teaghan says.

She's back at police headquarters at 8th and Race, the "Round-house," inside its cramped and outdated evidence lab. Officer Alex Sugar, the videographer who shot the footage at the Pancoast crime scene, cues everything up and then hesitates. His hand lingers over the mouse.

"You sure about this?" Alex asks.

"What do you mean?" Teaghan says. "Of course I'm sure. I need to see who was watching."

They're standing in front of a battered old monitor nearly two decades old, hooked up to a computer that's not much younger. Criminals can afford to treat themselves to the latest weapons and communications devices, but cops are often fighting them with tools from the previous century.

"I don't know," Alex says. "I thought maybe you wouldn't want to see him."

"See who?"

"Diaz," he says quietly. "You and Diaz are in the footage, too."

Teaghan hesitates but only for a moment. "It's fine. Roll it."

Alex is sweet for warning her. But seeing Diaz is the whole point of this. Because there's only one connection between the Diaz murders and the Pancoast murders. And that is Diaz himself, who was very visible at the crime scene that morning.

If the killer saw him, then the killer would have been standing in the crowd, watching them work.

Alex clicks the mouse, and on-screen the crowd outside the Pancoast home springs to life.

Police videographers often shoot footage of crowds outside the yellow tape, because a surprising number of perps love to return to the scenes of their own crimes. Teaghan is praying not only that the psycho she's hunting will have done the same thing but that he'll also have done something to make himself stand out.

If the killer caught a look at Diaz, that might explain how the nutcase tagged her partner as his next target.

"Pan left," she tells Alex.

But who could it be? There were easily two dozen people gathered on Christian Street that morning, a slice of South Philly life. Retirees, joggers, business types, hipsters, construction workers, parents with children...

"Wait. Stop right there."

Diaz left only one clue behind. The word *Daddy,* scrawled in his own blood on the living-room carpet. Was her partner trying to tell her something? Or was it merely the first word of a final message to his children? *Daddy's sorry.*

No. That wasn't Diaz. And Franny wasn't a killer.

Someone else in this crowd did this to them.

If the psycho saw Diaz, there's a good chance Diaz caught a glimpse of the psycho, too. And maybe even recognized him in the moments before his death.

Daddy.

It's not the start of an apology. He was trying to tell Teaghan who did it.

"Right there," Teaghan says, pointing at the screen. "Can you zoom in on this guy?"

"Who? The one with the baby?"

"Yeah."

The daddy, she thinks to herself.

Alex clicks the plus sign at the corner of the image, and slowly the footage zooms in on the daddy. With every jump in size, the image pixelates a bit more. But Teaghan can see he's a white male in his early forties, a bit of scruff on his cheeks and chin, and in need of a haircut.

And maybe it's the jagged image, but there's something weird about his clothes, too. Like he rolled out of bed that morning and strapped his baby to his chest to run errands before he had a chance to straighten himself up. Some house husbands really let themselves go. She was even starting to see it with Charlie, who sometimes went a day or two without showering. (Which, *ew,* Teaghan thinks. They're going to have to talk about that at some point.)

This guy with the baby, though, looks like he takes a very devil-may-care attitude toward personal hygiene. That poor baby. Imagine what he or she has to put up with all day long.

"Alex, can you give me a closer look at that kid? Like maybe a sharper glimpse of it from somewhere else in the footage?"

"*It*, huh?" Alex asks, bemused. "You're a new mom aren't you? I thought it was against the law to call a baby *it*."

"Believe me, I say far worse things at three a.m. when he's crying and won't go to sleep. Can you bring up another shot?"

"Sorry," Alex says, clicking the mouse. The footage rewinds, pushes forward, and rewinds again until Alex suddenly stops, his eye catching something in the still image.

"Ooh, I think this is a good one."

Alex clicks rapidly. "Bringing up baby," he says, unable to control the smirk on his face. But if Teaghan gets the joke, she gives no indication.

"Wait," Teaghan says, pointing. "Right there."

"What?"

"Push in on that. Can't you see it?"

Alex has to click the mouse a few more times before it becomes clear.

"That's no baby," Teaghan says.

CHAPTER 30

THE BLOOD IS EVERYWHERE.

I manage to plunge my trembling hands into the (icky luke-warm) blood to turn off the faucet and stop the flow, but the mess is already made, slopping over my pants and shoes now. What is going on here? Or worse, is something (someone) down there in all of that red?

I plunge my hands back into the disgustingly full tub, praying that my fingertips won't brush up against anything—*(like my sweet baby girl)*—at the bottom.

The more I feel around, the more I want to vomit. I'm in this stuff up to my elbows…now my upper arms, with my face only a few inches from the surface. The harsh, copper scent of the blood is all up in my nose and mouth and eyes. Human blood has the most distinctively horrifying aroma. Like it's nature's way of telling you that if you're surrounded by this much icky red stuff, then brother, you're in serious trouble.

Am I in serious trouble, though?

Where did all of this come from?

After much panicked searching, I'm thankful to find nothing

at the bottom of our tub. Man, I feel dizzy. I should go check on Jennifer in her crib, just to make sure, but I'm so overwhelmed by the sight of all of this watery human fluid that I stagger backward until I slip, and my tailbone slams against the hard tile floor.

Just give me a minute. I need a minute to breathe. A minute to process. To let the blood finish dripping from my arms.

I'm coming, baby girl. Daddy's coming. Daddy can't hold you with his arms covered in this horrible stuff.

But then I see something weird on the floor. (As if a blood-soaked bathroom wasn't weird enough.) Footprints. Not shoe-prints but the partial bloody prints of bare feet, leading away from the tub and toward the hallway.

How had I not noticed this before?

Part of me thinks Ruth is totally going to kill me when she sees this mess. But I need to figure out this insanity now and worry about Ruth later. I climb to my feet, sloshing in the bloody water, and follow the bloody prints.

I take a glance down at myself. I look like I've been working part-time in a meat-processing plant. Insane!

I'm careful not to smudge the mystery footprints (evidence, you know) as I track them out of the bathroom and down the hardwood staircase. As I head downstairs, I think about that plaque some people hang in their homes—you know, the one about the footprints and God carrying you on a sandy beach. I wonder what it means when *bloody* footprints suddenly appear next to yours.

Whatever it is, it can't be good.

The trail leads me through the living room, which is now completely empty, as if bandits cleared us out in the five minutes I was upstairs in the bathroom. Only that stupid tool bag and wastebasket remain. What the heck is going on?

Worry about it later, I tell myself. *You'll only understand if you follow the trail.*

Being a good father and husband means that you're supposed to be the rock of stability at the center of swirling chaos. So I refuse to surrender to the insanity. I will figure this out. Ruth and the kids are depending on me!

The trail leads to the back door, down the stairs, across our smallish backyard, through the fence, down an alley, and through the park. As I trudge through the grass, small gray squirrels dart around me, as if taunting me. Don't worry. I'll come back and deal with those little jerks later. All of them. If it means I have to buy dozens of small cages.

A barrel-chested mailman on his daily route does a double-take when he sees me walking by. I realize how I must look.

"Sorry," I tell him. "I know I'm a great big dripping mess. But I'm going through a bit of a personal crisis at home."

The mailman says nothing. It's as if he's been frozen in place, a thick bundle of bills in his hand.

"But don't worry, it's not my blood!" I quickly add, as if my explanation will put him at ease.

It doesn't. The mailman unfreezes, then abruptly turns a corner, either to continue his route or to call the men with the white van and the straitjackets.

Well, I can't worry about him now. I've got a mystery to solve.

And sure enough, the footprints continue, taking me all the way across the street and down to the grassy banks of the Schuylkill, before coming to an abrupt halt right at the river's chilly edge.

What the heck does all of this evidence mean? Did a blood-covered man use our bathroom, leave the tub water running, then proceed to steal all of our possessions before making a speedy river getaway?

You're so clueless, says a familiar voice. *As usual.*

I look up from the riverbank. There, standing waist deep in the water, is my sweet darling wife.

"Ruth! What are you doing in there?" I practically shout. "You're going to get sick!" Her face is so wan, so sad. What's happened to her?

You're the one who's sick, she says. *They're going to catch you. Very soon. I have it on good authority.*

"Ruth, please stop. This isn't funny! Do you have any idea of what I've been through today?"

Have you ever seen someone's eyes go completely black? Well, now imagine someone you love, someone you care about deeply and passionately, someone you've sworn to honor and obey forever. Imagine their eyes going black, to the point where you're not sure they're human anymore.

Don't tell me, she says, *about what* you've *been through.*

"This is crazy," I say. Then I pull off my shoes, roll up the bottoms of my trousers, and go wading into the river, intending to pull Ruth out by force if it comes to that. The water is freezing. I can practically feel all the pores on my legs squeezing shut. And let's not talk about what the bottom of the river feels like.

"Ruth, just stay where you are…"

But a few steps in, I realize she's gone.

And oh, look.

I'm the one who's bleeding.

CHAPTER 31

"ARE YOU SURE? Looks real enough to me."

Teaghan squints as she takes a closer look at the image on the screen. "Trust me, Alex. I just had one of these airlifted out of me. I'm kind of an expert on the subject. That baby is fake."

"Still can't see how you can tell."

"No baby stays still for that long. The question is, who's her daddy?"

Alex zooms in on the image as close as he can, and yeah, the baby, when seen from the right angle, is obviously fake. A good fake, mind you. Realistically sized and everything, the kind of expensive doll that little girls dress up and take to tea with their mommies. But the perfection is what tipped Teaghan off to the truth. Real babies don't act like props. They've got attitudes and impulses and agendas all their own.

Now the big question: what's this scruffy middle-aged dude doing with a fake doll strapped to his chest on the fringes of a crime scene?

You were trying to blend, right? Keep the attention off your face as you watched us—the cops working the murders you orchestrated.

After Alex prints out multiple headshots of Daddy from the Pancoast video, Teaghan circulates them throughout the department with a note attached: *Anybody recognize this guy? An ex-con, maybe? On a wanted list somewhere?*

Her fellow homicide detectives are very eager to take a look when she walks up and whispers to them face-to-face, "I think this is the scumbag who killed Diaz and his family."

Surprisingly few detectives push back on Teaghan. Instead, many of them voice a variation on the same theme: *I knew Franny couldn't have done this.*

Diaz, no matter his faults, is still a brother to them. And they want nothing more than to avenge his family.

Technically, the PD has access to facial-recognition software. But to use it, you have to ask the FBI for a favor, and depending on the political climate, the commissioner himself has to get involved. Teaghan has no patience for that nonsense. She prefers to do it old-school, no red tape. If this guy's a known scumbag, chances are someone in the department will recognize him.

And within twenty minutes, Teaghan has a hit.

But not on a killer.

Instead, someone recognizes a *victim*.

"Holy crap, I think that's Harry Posehn," says Detective D'Elia. "You know, the lawyer whose wife went nuts, then killed him and their kids? Happened just a couple of months ago."

Teaghan is nearly rocked back on her heels. W. Harold Posehn, the former defense attorney? The first familicide in the series?

"Wait, wait," she says. "I thought Posehn was dead."

D'Elia turns a bit sheepish. "Well, we found his blood all over the house, and it looked like he made it all the way down to the river before falling in and drowning," he says. "We figured the current carried him all the way down to the Navy Yard, maybe even the Delaware Bay."

"And this never made it to the press?" Teaghan says.

"No. Posehn's parents are pretty powerful in the state, and they wanted everything kept quiet. And they've got the mayor's ear, so…"

Parents, Teaghan thinks. *Harry Posehn is still alive.* He was a father—a *parent*—and he killed his wife and children. He framed his wife and escaped. But why would he murder them? Was it punishment? Did he think it was a merciful act?

Is that what he's doing now? Killing parents and children in families that he thinks are broken? Or is it revenge?

CHAPTER 32

THE WORLD IS what you make it.

That's what my daddy, Big Harold, always told me.

If you find yourself stuck in a life you don't want, that's no one's fault but your own.

Don't get me wrong. I loved Ruth and the kids. Madly. Deeply. I would have done anything for them. Why did they think I worked so many hours to provide them with all of the material comforts they deserved?

Sure, Ruth complained that I was never home, but I also knew she enjoyed the high-end appliances and Le Creuset cookware and the big town house with hardwood floors and a claw-foot tub big enough to bathe our entire family at once. What was I supposed to do? Quit the firm and tell her to live with less?

You know, it's kind of her fault, actually. Ruth should have told me something was wrong!

One day you get up and take your shower and drink your coffee and go to work, and you're there for, like, fourteen hours, and you're exhausted, and all you want to do is go home and enjoy a small meal and a glass of wine with your wife, but instead you find your wife in your bathroom, and she's…

Well, it's probably best not to dwell on the past.

Better to think about the future.

The future, where the possibilities are endless!

I mean, think about it. Just a few days ago, I didn't know her name at all. She was just a pretty face in the crowd. Tired eyes and bad posture, but oh, that glow in her cheeks. Unmistakable. I knew the moment I laid eyes on her that it would be fun to get to know her.

Her partner was another story. He didn't deserve to be in her presence. I wonder how she put up with his boorishness. Wonder how many times he hit on her, hoping for a quickie in the back of their car. Wonder if she ever gave in…

No. Not my girl. She wouldn't do something like that. Some things you can just tell.

She is the only one I am meant to be with. Even her name sounded magical when the CSI guy pronounced it.

Detectives Diaz and Beaumont? You got a sec?

Beaumont.

B-E-A-U-M-O-N-T.

CHAPTER 33

BY LATE AFTERNOON, a bone-tired Teaghan—her breasts full of milk and her C-section scar aching like crazy—finally trudges up the front steps of their apartment building.

Her day went on longer than she expected. When Teaghan woke up this morning, she thought she was just chasing down a wild lead. By noon, that wild lead had turned into hard evidence, enough to convince Teaghan's superiors that W. Harold Posehn was alive and well and busy murdering families all over Philadelphia.

Oh, won't his proud parents be surprised.

By 2:00 p.m., SWAT teams were combing Posehn's old neighborhood and the banks of the Schuylkill River for miles in both directions. Police choppers covered the scene from the air. After they sealed Kelly Drive—the popular riverfront drive that offered a quick way out of downtown—traffic began to snarl all over the city. A lot of people were going to be furious later today when their commute home turned into a long, grinding slog.

And sure, the old Teaghan Beaumont would have liked to be in the thick of the hunt, wanting nothing more than to hear the satisfying double click of handcuffs around this psycho's wrists.

But the new Teaghan, the detective who is also a mom, just wants to hold her son and maybe get a little sleep.

She pushes the key into the lock of their front door and calls out, "Mommy's home."

Still so weird to say that.

Because of the strange, narrow layout of the apartment, the front door leads down a long hallway to the living room proper. Teaghan likes to think of the hallway as her decompression chamber. Leave the cop stuff at the door, and slowly transform back into wife—and now mother—as she walks through the passage.

This rarely works, mind you. Even before she had Christopher, Teaghan couldn't help but drag the cop stuff into their living space, into their kitchen, even into their bedroom. She can't count the times Charlie has asked her what she was thinking about, and she'd have to lie and say *Nothing*. Because most times, she was thinking about something incredibly grisly from a recent crime scene. Even after their more intimate moments.

Now, as Teaghan approaches the living room, she hears the baby wailing. Oh, boy. So much for decompression.

"I'm coming, sweetie, hang on," she says, pulling her gun from its holster. "Mommy's gotta put her work tools away."

Charlie and Teaghan argued over where to store her gun, now that there was a child in the apartment. Finally, they decided on a lockbox in the topmost kitchen cabinet—at least, until little

Christopher is up and walking around. Then they'll have to figure out some other place. "Maybe that's when we start thinking about a house," Charlie said.

She deferred that conversation until later. "Let's just get through the trauma of being new parents first," she said.

Teaghan reaches up to the top cabinet and opens the door. Which causes a bit of pain, stretching like this, especially with her scars still aching and her breasts ready to burst.

The baby's loud wails make them ache even more.

"So how was your day, Charlie? Get a lot of words done?"

But nothing.

Weird that her husband doesn't reply. Usually, he's eagerly handing off the kid like a hot potato. Is it possible he's fallen asleep and somehow doesn't hear the baby bawling his eyes out?

Teaghan pulls down the lockbox, flips the combination, opens it.

"Charlie?"

CHAPTER 34

IT'S BEEN QUITE a while since I've held a real baby.

Not since my sweet baby girl Jennifer, a little more than six weeks ago. Which, admittedly, feels like a lifetime ago.

And now it is time for a new life.

I hold this baby, a gorgeous little boy, and don't even care that he's screaming his head off. Babies do that. I know, I was guilty of being impatient when the boys were younger, and I would yell at Ruth for not being able to keep them quiet. But I know better now. When you know better, you do better.

"It's okay, Christopher," I murmur, trying to keep my strange-sounding voice as soothing as possible. I know babies are able to hear their parents' voices from the womb, and no doubt he's gotten used to the sound of his biological father. But that's okay. Babies are adaptive. He'll get to know mine.

"Won't you, Christopher?" I coo.

I know his name because there's a banner in his nursery—probably purchased by coworkers or in-laws. WELCOME CHRISTOPHER, it proudly proclaims. I wish I could have been there for the birth. Well, with enough time and photos, I suppose, it will eventually feel like I *was* there.

Breaking into a police officer's home was surprisingly easy. Old brownstone mansions like this have basement windows, just like in my former home. It didn't take much muscle to pry open the lock and shimmy into the basement, which turned out to be the floor with the bedrooms.

(This won't do, by the way. I'll have to bring my new family to a suitable home, one where the floors aren't all mixed up.)

The former husband and father—I don't know his name and don't care to learn it now—was busy typing on his laptop with his big dumb mitts when I crept into the master bedroom. He didn't have a chance, the sorry slob.

I don't even think the guy bothered to shower today. Kids notice that sort of thing. If you don't put in the effort, what makes you think they will?

Shameful, really. Looks like I showed up just in time.

I looked down at his body, now sprawled out awkwardly, and told him, "That's what you get for taking your eye off the ball. Parenting is not a hobby, buddy boy. It's a full-time commitment."

And then I picked up my new son for the first time.

Oh, that moment. I wish you could have been there to take a photo.

The whole idea was to surprise Detective Beaumont, B-E-A-U-M-O-N-T, though I should probably start referring to her as Teaghan. It would be silly to call my new wife by her last name.

Come to think of it, Beaumont is probably her married name. I'll have her change it. Teaghan Posehn has an interesting ring to it, don't you think? Though, sadly, I'll probably need a new surname, too.

"What do you think, Christopher?" I murmur now. "What would you like your last name to be? Something that goes nicely with Chris, I think. This is all for you, my little prince."

Christopher wails in response, but that's okay. He'll appreciate all of my efforts someday.

So I rock him and sit on the couch—nothing more than a futon, actually, which will also have to go. Can't have little Chris climbing all over a futon, pinching his fingers in the hinges.

"How about a big overstuffed sofa, my man? Something for all three of us to curl up on while we watch TV."

And then…

CLACK.

I hear it.

"Mommy's home," a voice calls out, and it's the most beautiful voice I've ever heard. The kind of voice a man could learn to love. Already, this whole thing feels so right.

(Sorry, Ruth, but it's the truth. You could be a little abrasive.)

And I know what you're going to say. That I'm going to repeat my mistakes and work too much and not make time for my family. But I swear, hand on the Bible, I am going to change.

"I'm coming, sweetie, hang on," the sweet voice says. It's even closer now. Just beyond the doorway. "Mommy's gotta put her work tools away."

Our baby cries even harder at the sound of his mother's voice. He knows something exciting is about to happen. He can't wait for his new life to begin! It's going to be so amazing.

"So how was your day, Charlie? Get a lot of words done?"

Charlie. Feh. So that was the loser's name. Well, sorry, Charlie, this ship is about to set sail. Thanks for the biological contribution to our little family.

"Charlie?"

Come on inside, Detec—Teaghan. My love. Step through that door. I know, at first this whole thing may be a bit of a shock.

Believe me, I get it.

Which is why I've brought my gun, just to make sure you don't do anything rash. Once you hear me out, you'll agree that I'm giving you the opportunity of a lifetime.

Don't worry, Christopher. Here comes Mommy....

CHAPTER 35

AT FIRST, TEAGHAN doesn't quite know how to process the image before her eyes.

W. Harold Posehn—the psychotic killer the entire city is searching for right this very moment—is calmly perched on her living-room futon. Baby Christopher is in his arms, bawling his eyes out.

"Hi, honey," Posehn says over the noise. "Welcome home."

There's a gun in his hand, held as casually as a baby bottle or a pacifier. But the barrel is very much pointed at her.

Is this a nightmare? Has she stepped into an alternate universe? No.

Because if this psycho could easily read Diaz's name, then he could read hers, too. She's merely next on his list.

Teaghan wants to scream, *Hand over my son!* But that's the mom inside her. The detective inside her takes over, because she's the only one who can possibly save them all.

"Mr. Posehn," Teaghan says. "I'll admit, I'm a little surprised to see you here."

"Please, call me Will. The whole initial and middle name thing was for my father, Harold. I never liked it. But sometimes you end up doing things to make your parents happy."

"Don't I know it," Teaghan says, forcing an easygoing smile onto a face that wants to scream. "Hey, my baby's really upset. You mind passing him over to me so I can, you know, give him the breast?"

"Not yet," Posehn says. "I want to make a few things clear first."

It's impossibly hard for Teaghan to swallow her anger, but she says, "Okay."

She glances at the gun. Is this what he used to threaten Franny into shooting her family? Because that's the only way it made sense. Franny loved her husband and her family; there's no way she'd turn a gun on her own flesh and blood. She'd sooner gnaw her own hands off at the wrist.

I'll get him for you, Franny, she thinks. *Destroy him for what he did to your family.*

"I know Christopher here is crying his little lungs out," Posehn is saying, "but I'm actually great with kids. I mean, I *could* be great with kids."

"He's really hungry," Teaghan says. "Please let me feed him."

"Not yet!" Posehn snaps. "Let me finish." He sighs, then shakes his head, as if trying to collect his thoughts. "I know you're a busy career woman. I took one look at you at the crime scene on Christian Street and thought to myself, now, there's a woman who's dedicated to her profession. As a former workaholic lawyer, I can appreciate that."

"What about Ruth?" Teaghan asks. "Didn't she appreciate how hard you worked?"

Posehn recoils, as if her very name is a slap in the face. "She kept secrets from me," he says quietly. "She should have told me…"

"Told you what?"

"We were building a life together. And then one day she decided to throw it all away. She had no right to do that."

"So you punished her. Just like you punished the Cookes and the Pancoasts and my partner's family."

Posehn doesn't react for a moment, as if his brain is a computer that's slipped into sleep mode. Then he blinks and snaps back. "The Cookes? Oh, if you'd met those insufferable people, you would have begged me to punish them yourself. You should have heard them complaining before dinner. Eh, I don't like that. Or wah, why does Jay get to use the BMW tonight, or boo-hoo, I'm only going to be able to spend six weeks down the shore instead of the whole summer. You should have heard them."

"That didn't mean they had to die."

"Oh, yes, they did. They weren't a family. They were breeding monsters. And those monsters would have gone on to breed more monsters, and the entire world would have been overrun."

"So you killed them."

Teaghan—still the detective, still trained to exact a confession out of a scumbag, even though they weren't in an interrogation room. Oh, how she wished they were in one of those rooms rather than right here, in the heart of her home.

"*I* didn't kill them," Posehn says. "Mommy Eleanor did. I merely hid in the pantry until it was time to add just the right *spice* to the soup. It was an autumn vegetable bisque with crispy prosciutto, by the way, very earthy, which made it easy to sneak a little arsenic into the mix. Isn't that how old ladies kill people? I thought so."

"And then you stuck around to finish her off with some painkillers. Did you have to force-feed them to her? Or was she already in shock after watching her entire family die?"

Posehn sighs in exasperation. "Point is, I'm done with all of that. I just want to be a house husband. All I want is to take care of this baby, and take care of you, in a way you both deserve. A way your former husband couldn't provide."

Former husband? Oh, no... Charlie...

Teaghan feels her muscles turn into steel cords. If this psycho has hurt her husband, she's going to utterly destroy him.

"What did you *do* to him?"

"Don't think about that right now," Posehn says. "I want you to open your mind and think about the possibility of us. It's not as crazy as it sounds."

But Teaghan is not thinking about *us.* She's thinking about the lockbox on her kitchen counter.

And how she's very, very happy that she didn't put her service revolver into it before stepping into the living room.

CHAPTER 36

I DON'T KNOW if I'm reaching her.

After all, Teaghan's a cop; she's trained to pretend. I've seen plenty of cops on the witness stand who deserve an Academy Award. They promise they're going to help you out and be your friend right up to the moment they swab the crook of your arm and prepare to jab you with the lethal injection.

But it's important that Teaghan believes me. Otherwise, this evening will have to go a very different way. And trust me, nobody wants that. Least of all me. With all of this work I've put into this new relationship so far, I'd hate to have to start all over again.

"What do you think, Teaghan?" I ask.

"If you want there to be an *us,*" Teaghan says, looking me right in the eyes, "then let me feed the baby so we can talk in peace."

And for a microsecond there, I totally believe her. She's *that* good. Her bright eyes lock with mine, telling me that we're practically man and wife already. And the baby in my arms is really ours. So sure, why wouldn't I let her breastfeed him? It's the most natural thing in the world. What am I saying? It's perhaps the most beautiful moment between a woman and a child, and I'll be privileged to be able to see it.

"That's it," she says quietly. "Give him to me."

But then I see her right hand dart toward the small of her back. And I see the slight grimace on her face, because the movement clearly hurts.

The C-section scars, you see. They're probably still tender. I saw it when she moved around the crime scene on Christian Street. It hurt her to move.

And I'll bet anything she hasn't practiced drawing her gun since enduring the surgery. She didn't realize how much it would hurt.

Probably nothing in comparison to how much it hurts me right now. All of my dreams, dashed in an instant. Just like they were six weeks ago. Why is it so hard to be a parent these days?

Oh, well. I guess this evening *is* going the other way.

I sigh and squeeze the trigger.

CHAPTER 37

THE BULLET CATCHES Teaghan in her upper arm and propels her body backward, slamming her against the living-room wall.

What's strange is that Christopher immediately stops crying, even as the shot is still echoing off the apartment walls. The explosion must have been deafening to his tiny ears. It either shocked him into silence or blew out his eardrums.

The pain in Teaghan's body is unreal, as if someone has swung a sledgehammer straight into her bicep, crushing bone and immediately numbing her limb all the way down to her fingertips.

She's never been shot before. The very idea always filled her with an existential kind of dread, because her Job is all about putting herself between innocent civilians and the guns of very bad men. Sometimes she would lie awake at night, thinking about what it would feel like.

But much to her surprise, the pain is nothing compared to what she experienced during childbirth and the aftermath of abdominal surgery.

And you know what? It's nothing compared to the white-hot rage she's feeling now.

While it was the detective who tried to talk her way out of this horrible situation, it is the mom inside Teaghan who now reaches her left hand toward the small of her back and grabs the handle of the revolver. Because the mom in Teaghan will do anything to protect her family.

Including aiming the gun with a hand she's never practiced with before and squeezing the trigger.

Blood sprays from Posehn's right shoulder, mere inches over her baby boy's head. The gun drops from Posehn's hand and falls onto the hardwood floor with a thump.

"Ow!" Posehn screams, not so much in agony as at the utter betrayal. "H-h-how could you? I wanted to give you everything! And this is how you treat me? Without even *talking* to me?"

The psycho puts his other hand around the baby's neck. Christopher's head looks so tiny next to Posehn's adult fingers.

Teaghan screams, aims, and fires again, this time placing a bullet in Posehn's left shoulder. His hand falls away from Christopher, and his whole body begins to writhe on the futon, unable to move either arm now, snarling at her.

"I'll do the same thing to you that I did to Ruth. You ask her. Then you'll see what happens when you defy me!"

Baby Christopher, still in shell-shocked silence, begins to slide down the psycho's legs, headed for the edge of his knees.

Teaghan drops her revolver and falls to her own knees, biting her tongue to keep from passing out. She lunges forward with her one good arm and pushes out with her legs....

Her baby is screaming and falling…

But Mommy's hand is there to break the worst of his fall.

She pulls him close to her, not feeling any pain at all now.

The very touch of him, the smell of him, is all the anesthetic she needs.

CHAPTER 38

TEAGHAN HOLDS HER baby boy close as they go looking for Daddy.

The psycho is passed out on their futon, most likely from the shock and blood loss, and Teaghan has already called it in. She expects uniformed officers to be knocking down her front door in a matter of minutes.

But there's one thing she's not going to let happen, and that is having someone else tell her what happened to Charlie. She needs to see it with her own eyes.

So she heads down the wooden steps to the basement, her legs extremely shaky beneath her body weight. *Please don't let me pass out,* she prays. *Let me keep it together long enough to see him one last time.*

Christopher, perhaps picking up on his mother's fear, begins to fuss again.

"It's okay, baby boy," she whispers. "Everything will be okay."

Not believing it herself, but sometimes a parent has to be the rock in this kind of situation.

She steadies herself against the doorframe and peers inside.

Charlie's body is in their bedroom, sprawled across their bed, his hair wet with blood. His open laptop is on the floor, splayed open like a plastic butterfly. He was probably writing, taking advantage of the baby's napping, when the psycho broke in and surprised him mid-sentence.

Her poor, sweet husband.

Your former husband…

CHAPTER 39

TEAGHAN HOLDS HER breath and grabs her husband's wrist, expecting it to be cold, expecting the emotional dam to burst any second now.

Instead, Charlie stirs, moaning, waking up, his hands flapping around like dying fish, trying to make sense of his surroundings.

"Ssss'okay," he says. "I'm up, I'm up, I'll get the baby…"

"Charlie!" Teaghan exclaims.

Baby Christopher looks at his mother in surprise. He's never heard her use that tone of voice before.

Teaghan can't lift her husband and hold her baby at the same time, so she goes for the next-best thing, crawling into bed next to him, the baby between them. She knows this won't last for long. For one thing, it hurts like crazy to put any kind of pressure on her right arm. For another, her colleagues will be here soon, in full force, and they're all going to have to be transported to the hospital. And the doctors are going to have one hell of a fight on their hands if they think they're going to take Christopher away from her for even a second.

"Sweetie," Charlie says, still dazed, his eyes finally locking onto his wife. He smiles like a goof. "You're home early."

When Mitchum's beloved fourteen-year-old cousin is abducted, he must call on every lethal skill to track her down – but nothing is what it seems . . .

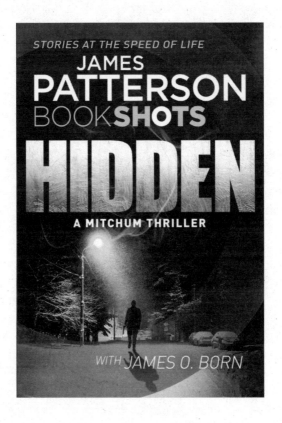

STORIES AT THE SPEED OF LIFE

JAMES
PATTERSON
BOOK**SHOTS**

HIDDEN

A MITCHUM THRILLER

WITH *JAMES O. BORN*

Read on for an extract

MY MOODY MONGREL, Bart Simpson, kept watch from the warm back-seat. He rarely found my job interesting. At least not this job.

I was next to the loading dock, folding newspapers for delivery. A surly driver named Nick dropped them off for me every morning at 5:50 sharp. What he lacked in personality he made up for in silence. I always said hello and never got an answer. Not even a "Hey, Mitchum." It was a good working relationship.

Even with the wind off the Hudson, I could crack a sweat moving the heavy bundles of papers. I used the knife I had gotten in the Navy to cut the straps holding them. My station wagon sagged under the weight of a full load. My two-day-a-week afternoon gig in Milton didn't strain the shocks nearly as bad. I usually dropped Bart off at my mom's then. My dog was as close to a grandchild as she had, and they could both complain about me.

In the early morning gloom, I caught a movement out of the corner of my eye and reacted quickly, turning with the knife still in my right hand. It was an instinct I couldn't explain. I was raised in upstate New York, not Bosnia. But I relaxed as soon as I saw

Albany Al, one of the few homeless people in Marlboro, standing near the loading dock, a dozen feet away.

The older man's whiskers spread as he grinned and rubbed his hand across his white beard. "Hello, Mitchum. They say you can never sneak up on a Navy SEAL. I guess that's true."

I was past the point of explaining to people that I was never an actual SEAL.

When I took a closer look at the old man, I realized he wasn't ready for the burst of arctic air that had descended on us. "Al, grab my extra coat from the car. It's too cold to be wandering around dressed like that."

"I couldn't."

"Go ahead. My cousin usually wears it, but she didn't show today. She's a wuss for avoiding the cold."

"I wondered where Bailey Mae was. I was hoping she had some of her coffee cake."

Then I realized the older man hadn't come to keep me company. He'd wandered over to snag some of Bailey Mae's famous coffee cake, which she handed out like business cards.

I said, "I miss her cake, too."

The old man said, "I can tell." He cackled as he rubbed his belly, but he was looking at me.

I patted my own belly and said, "It's my portable insulation." Maybe I hadn't been working out as hard as usual. A few warm days and some running would solve that.

The old man continued to cackle as he walked away with my coat.

WHEN I'D FINISHED my route, I headed over to my office off Route 9. At least, my unofficial office. I always hit Tina's Plentiful at about 8:15, right between the early breakfast crowd and late risers. The old diner sat in an empty strip mall that hadn't been updated since 1988. A couple of framed posters of the California coast hung on the walls. No one had ever explained their significance, and none of the customers seemed to care. The place had the best Reubens and tuna melts in upstate New York, and they treated me like family. Maybe it was because one of my cousins worked in the kitchen.

The lone waitress, Mabel, named by a mean-spirited mother, lit up when I walked in. Usually I sat in the rear booth to eat and see if I had any pressing business. There was never much pressing in Marlboro. Today I headed toward the counter since there wasn't much going on and it would make it easier on Mabel.

Mabel was a town favorite for her easy smile and the way she took time to chat with everyone who came into the diner. As soon as I sat down she said, "Finally, a friendly face."

I gave her a wink and said, "Is the world not treating Miss Teenage New York well today?"

"Funny. You should cheer me up by taking me to the movies in Newburgh one night."

"Only if my cousin Bailey Mae comes with us."

"Why?"

"So you understand it's as friends and not a date."

"Am I so terrible? You've had some tough breaks and I'm a lot of fun."

I couldn't help a smile. "Of course you're not so terrible. You're also so *young*. And I'm not going to be the guy who holds you back from all the suitable young men in the area." That was as much as I wanted to say today.

Before she could answer, I glanced out the wide front window and saw my cousin Alice, Bailey Mae's mom, hustling across the street toward the diner. She is a year older than me and was only twenty when Bailey Mae was born. She is a good mom, and the rest of us help. Her usual smile was nowhere to be seen as her long brown hair flapped in the wind behind her. She yanked open the door and rushed right to me.

"Mitchum, Bailey Mae is missing."

Suddenly, the day got colder.

I SPENT A few minutes trying to calm Alice down as we started to check some of the places Bailey Mae liked to hang out. Bailey Mae hadn't been to school that day or to the library or to the sad little arcade where she sometimes played out-of-date games. Alice had gone to sleep early the night before, after her shift at the bottling factory in Gardnertown. Bailey Mae usually came home about eight o'clock. She's a smart fourteen-year-old, and a quarter of the town is related to her.

We wandered around town, asking a few questions. No one thought it was unusual, because I am the unofficial private investigator for the whole area.

Mrs. Hoffman on Dubois Street hadn't seen Bailey Mae but took the time to thank me for finding her son, who had been on a bender in Albany and didn't have the cash to get home.

After nearly an hour, I tracked down Timmy Jones, a buddy of mine from high school who now worked for the Ulster sheriff's office.

Timmy raised his hands, showing his thick fingers, and said, "I spoke with your cousin Alice already. We're making a few checks, but Bailey Mae has wandered off before."

I knew she sometimes got frustrated and left the house, but she usually ended up at my house or my mom's house. I said, "She's a good girl."

"No one's saying she's not. But we can't just call out the troops every time a teenager is out past curfew or mad at their parents."

"Bailey Mae is more responsible. She wouldn't do something like that."

Finally Timmy said, "Okay, we'll get everyone out looking for her. But get your family involved, too. There's more of them than there are cops in the area."

BAILEY MAE HAS always been my favorite relative, and I have plenty to choose from in Marlboro. After I rounded a few up and explained the situation, the look on my cousin Todd's face said it all: they were worried. Bailey Mae is the family's shining light. Todd is a self-centered dick, and even he was concerned enough for our little cousin that he closed his precious auto repair shop to help search.

I pulled Alice aside and hit her with some simple questions about what was going on around the house, what the last thing she said to Bailey Mae was, and whether they'd been fighting. The usual.

She said, "I told you everything. There were no problems. I haven't been drinking and she hasn't been angry. The only thing that's new is that she's been hanging out with Natty a little bit."

That caught me by surprise. I blurted out, "Natty, as in my brother, Nathaniel?"

Alice nodded. "No real reason for it. He's nice to her and she likes his car. That's all I ever hear about. You know teenagers and cars. Just another crazy dream of hers."

"Natty shouldn't be anywhere near Bailey Mae."

Alice said, "He did his time."

"He always does. But he's still a drug dealer."

"He's family."

"Maybe by New York State law, but not the way I see it."

I PURPOSELY LEFT Alice in Marlboro when I made my way down to Newburgh. My old station wagon sputtered a couple of times but got me there in about twenty minutes. Route 9 was open this time of day and I parked directly in front of the State of Mind Tavern, just past the I-84 underpass, the dive bar where Natty, my older brother, does business. I immediately spotted his leased sports car on the side of the dingy building. Natty had gotten tired of having cars seized every time some industrious cop stopped him and found dope inside. All it took was enough weight to be charged for trafficking and the car became part of the crime—and also part of police inventory up for auction. So now he switched out cars every year. The hot little convertible was near the end of its term.

As I opened the door, the bartender looked up through the haze. They aren't as strict in upstate as they are in the city, so cigarette smoke hung in the air. The smell of toaster pizza was permanently stuck in the discolored wallpaper. The bartender, who looked like he dined on steroids every day, gave me a cursory look and deemed me unworthy of an acknowledgment.

My brother, Nathaniel, or "Natty" as he's been called his whole life, is two inches shorter than me, at six feet even, and thin as a rail from a life of drugs, coffee, and cigarettes. I had no clue why he got called Natty while I've been called by my last name, Mitchum, since childhood. Only our mom calls me by my first name.

His head jerked up instantly. Instinct from his line of work. We have the same blue eyes and prominent jawline, but not much else in common.

I headed directly toward him when the bartender, who doubled as Natty's bodyguard, stepped from behind the bar to grab my left arm. Now he wanted to dance; a second ago he was too good to speak to me. A quick twist and thumb lock with my right hand dropped the ox to one knee in pain until the man understood how stupid his idea had been. Thank you, SEAL basic training class 406.

Natty stood up quickly and said, "Tony, no need for that. This is my little brother." He moved around the table to greet me, rushing past Angel, his semi-regular girlfriend, who once posed for *Penthouse* or one of those magazines.

I held up my hand and said, "Save it."

That brought Natty up short. "Why? What's wrong? Is it Mom?"

"Where's Bailey Mae?"

"Bailey Mae? I haven't seen her in a couple of days. Why?"

"She's missing and I heard she's been hanging out around you. You're a shithead so I came here first."

"How could you suspect me of doing anything to our own cousin? I love that girl. She's got dreams."

"We all do."

Natty stepped closer and said, "Look, Mitchum, I know you don't like what I do, but it's only a little pot and I don't force anyone into anything." He put his arm around my shoulder and started to lead me back toward the front door.

I stopped short and grabbed his arm. The bartender saw his chance at some payback, stepped forward, and took a swing at my head with his ham fist. It might as well have happened in slow motion, given all my years of preparation and the months of Navy training. It was almost an insult. I bobbed back a few inches and the big man's fist passed me. Then I swung Natty into him like a bag of potatoes, and they fell back into the barstools and got hopelessly tangled together on the grimy floor.

Another guy who'd been sitting at Natty's table grabbed a pool cue and stepped forward. In an instant I had my Navy knife out of my pocket and flipped open. I needed to blow off some steam and had just now realized it. As I'd expected, the jerk focused all of his attention on the knife, so I landed a perfect front kick in his gut, knocking him off his feet. To give the guy credit, he was upright and holding the pool cue again in a flash, his face beet red from the shock of being kicked and the momentary lack of oxygen.

Natty scrambled off the floor, his hands up, and jumped between me and the guy with the pool cue. Natty yelled, "Wait,

wait!" He turned toward the other man and said, "Chuck, chill out!" He changed tone and attitude as he turned toward me. "Mitchum, just calm down and put the knife away. I want to help."

I had never heard my brother say that to anyone. Ever.

JAMES PATTERSON

BOOK**SHOTS**

OUT THIS MONTH

HIDDEN: A MITCHUM THRILLER

Rejected by the Navy SEALs, Mitchum is content to be his small town's unofficial private eye, until his beloved 14-year-old cousin is abducted. Now he'll call on every lethal skill to track her down . . .

THE HOUSE HUSBAND

Detective Teaghan Beaumont is getting closer and closer to discovering the truth about Darien Marshall. But there's a twist that she – and you, dear reader – will never see coming.

EXQUISITE: THE DIAMOND TRILOGY, PART 3

Siobhan and Derick's relationship has been a rollercoaster ride that has pushed Derick too far. Will Siobhan be able to win back her soul mate?

KISSES AT MIDNIGHT (ebook only)

Three exciting romances – *The McCullagh Inn in Maine*, *Sacking the Quarterback* and *Seducing Shakespeare*.

SEDUCING SHAKESPEARE (ebook only)

William Shakespeare has fallen in love – with the beautiful Marietta DiSonna. But what Shakespeare doesn't know is that Marietta is acting a role. Unless Shakespeare can seduce her in return . . .

BOOK**SHOTS**

STORIES AT THE SPEED OF LIFE

www.bookshots.com

ALSO BY JAMES PATTERSON

ALEX CROSS NOVELS
Along Came a Spider
Kiss the Girls
Jack and Jill
Cat and Mouse
Pop Goes the Weasel
Roses are Red
Violets are Blue
Four Blind Mice
The Big Bad Wolf
London Bridges
Mary, Mary
Cross
Double Cross
Cross Country
Alex Cross's Trial (*with Richard DiLallo*)
I, Alex Cross
Cross Fire
Kill Alex Cross
Merry Christmas, Alex Cross
Alex Cross, Run
Cross My Heart
Hope to Die
Cross Justice
Cross the Line

THE WOMEN'S MURDER CLUB SERIES
1st to Die
2nd Chance (*with Andrew Gross*)
3rd Degree (*with Andrew Gross*)
4th of July (*with Maxine Paetro*)
The 5th Horseman (*with Maxine Paetro*)
The 6th Target (*with Maxine Paetro*)
7th Heaven (*with Maxine Paetro*)
8th Confession (*with Maxine Paetro*)
9th Judgement (*with Maxine Paetro*)
10th Anniversary (*with Maxine Paetro*)
11th Hour (*with Maxine Paetro*)
12th of Never (*with Maxine Paetro*)
Unlucky 13 (*with Maxine Paetro*)
14th Deadly Sin (*with Maxine Paetro*)
15th Affair (*with Maxine Paetro*)

DETECTIVE MICHAEL BENNETT SERIES
Step on a Crack (*with Michael Ledwidge*)
Run for Your Life (*with Michael Ledwidge*)
Worst Case (*with Michael Ledwidge*)
Tick Tock (*with Michael Ledwidge*)
I, Michael Bennett (*with Michael Ledwidge*)
Gone (*with Michael Ledwidge*)
Burn (*with Michael Ledwidge*)
Alert (*with Michael Ledwidge*)
Bullseye (*with Michael Ledwidge*)

PRIVATE NOVELS
Private (*with Maxine Paetro*)
Private London (*with Mark Pearson*)
Private Games (*with Mark Sullivan*)
Private: No. 1 Suspect (*with Maxine Paetro*)
Private Berlin (*with Mark Sullivan*)
Private Down Under (*with Michael White*)

Private L.A. (*with Mark Sullivan*)
Private India (*with Ashwin Sanghi*)
Private Vegas (*with Maxine Paetro*)
Private Sydney (*with Kathryn Fox*)
Private Paris (*with Mark Sullivan*)
The Games (*with Mark Sullivan*)
Private Delhi (*with Ashwin Sanghi*)

NYPD RED SERIES

NYPD Red (*with Marshall Karp*)
NYPD Red 2 (*with Marshall Karp*)
NYPD Red 3 (*with Marshall Karp*)
NYPD Red 4 (*with Marshall Karp*)

STAND-ALONE THRILLERS

Sail (*with Howard Roughan*)
Swimsuit (*with Maxine Paetro*)
Don't Blink (*with Howard Roughan*)
Postcard Killers (*with Liza Marklund*)
Toys (*with Neil McMahon*)
Now You See Her (*with Michael Ledwidge*)
Kill Me If You Can (*with Marshall Karp*)
Guilty Wives (*with David Ellis*)
Zoo (*with Michael Ledwidge*)
Second Honeymoon (*with Howard Roughan*)
Mistress (*with David Ellis*)
Invisible (*with David Ellis*)
The Thomas Berryman Number
Truth or Die (*with Howard Roughan*)
Murder House (*with David Ellis*)
Never Never (*with Candice Fox*)
Woman of God (*with Maxine Paetro*)

BOOKSHOTS

Black & Blue (*with Candice Fox*)
Break Point (*with Lee Stone*)
Cross Kill
Private Royals (*with Rees Jones*)
The Hostage (*with Robert Gold*)
Zoo 2 (*with Max DiLallo*)
Heist (*with Rees Jones*)
Hunted (*with Andrew Holmes*)
Airport: Code Red (*with Michael White*)
The Trial (*with Maxine Paetro*)
Little Black Dress (*with Emily Raymond*)
Chase (*with Michael Ledwidge*)
Let's Play Make-Believe (*with James O. Born*)
Dead Heat (*with Lee Stone*)
Triple Threat
113 Minutes (*with Max DiLallo*)
The Verdict (*with Robert Gold*)
French Kiss (*with Richard DiLallo*)
$10,000,000 Marriage Proposal (*with Hilary Liftin*)
Kill or Be Killed
Taking the Titanic (*with Scott Slaven*)
Killer Chef (*with Jeffrey J. Keyes*)
Taking the Titanic (*with Scott Slaven*)
Kidnapped (*with Robert Gold*)
Killer Chef (*with Jeffrey J. Keyes*)
The Christmas Mystery (*with Richard DiLallo*)
Come and Get Us (*with Shan Serafin*)